BODY IN THE COVE

A WARM SPRINGS MYSTERY
BOOK FOUR

D. SMITH

Body in the Cove by D. Smith

Book 4 in the Warm Springs Mystery series

Published by Kingfisher Press

Fairview, North Carolina, United States of America

Visit the author's website at www.douglaspsmith.com

Cover design by Getcovers

Print ISBN: 978-1-964344-06-5

CHAPTER ONE

Getting shot was a great way to focus me on who pulled the trigger. They would have plenty of additional opportunities, and I'd prefer they did not. After leaving the hospital with my superficial neck wound, Bryan had briefed me on what they had found. It was not much, but was all I had to work with from the shooting itself. My list of known potential suspects was too large to do much with. And as I had told Bryan, the number of potential unknown suspects was even larger. I had made an impression in Warm Springs and Hamilton County, but perhaps not one conducive to my long-term health.

Meanwhile, I had other issues to deal with. Feeding Kat, attending the bookstore, tending the community garden, and buying groceries were just a few of my life's regular requirements. I also had special projects, such as searching for my assassin, finding a way to shut down Benjamin Rawley, and researching the letter found under the cottage that detailed three murders.

It was a nice fall day, but instead of enjoying it on campus, I needed to begin my distasteful chore list. I decided to tackle the easiest special project first.

Benjamin Rawley, the long-time flunky working for the state, had decided he did not like me. It was very mutual. But I did not take it personally since he literally disliked everyone in Warm Springs from what I could tell. The feeling from Warm Springs towards him was also mutual. Yet no one had taken a shot at him, so I guess I was less liked than Benjamin. Sobering, but it was an environment I was familiar with due to past actions that usually ended up with me disliked. But it had not been a problem for me until Ison told me that Benjamin was up to his old tricks. He was trying to have all the trees on campus cut down because he could get a cut of the profits. Plus, he might get the campus garden shut down just because he was a jerk.

I needed help to get something major on Benjamin that would not allow him to use his powerful friends in Atlanta to continue protecting him. I thought I knew the right person for the job. I drove over to Hamilton, the county seat of Hamilton County. I parked near the courthouse and walked to a small but nice office. There was no longer any sign on the post outside, and a light spot on the building itself showed where another sign had once been.

I was at the office of Lawrence K. Endicott, IV, formerly called Larry the Lawless because he did not do much obvious lawyering, despite his office's proximity to the courthouse. Instead, his specialty had been setting up shell companies and other legal devices for crooks all around the region. Then he was caught with a brick of marijuana and $100,000 in unexplained cash. Knowing he was framed, and likely by one of his clients, he gave away most of his secrets to the authorities. His penance was probation and disbarment, thus the lack of signs at his office.

I was the one who framed Larry, and I told him afterward. He was not happy about what I had done, but he realized he was leading a brief life, as any day one of his clients, or a competitor of a client, was likely to shoot him. Even before his arrest, criminal organizations under investigation for various prior wrongdoings were getting their corporate shells unraveled by the feds. The criminals would not take a chance of Larry flipping on them. Now he had flipped on all of them en masse, and he was possibly still in danger despite assurances from the state and federal authorities. But altogether he was in a better place with all the stress of his previous life gone. He had inherited the office, money, a house and some land, so he did not need to continue earning. But he still felt compelled to visit his office several times a week.

I walked in and sat in a comfortable chair across from his desk. His receptionist had departed immediately after his arrest.

"Hey Larry."

"Hi James. You just happened to be in the neighborhood today?"

"Something like that."

"Did you do the bookstore deal?" Larry asked.

"Yes, and thanks for reviewing the papers. Here is your fee." I opened my wallet and handed Larry a crisp one-dollar bill, his usual fee. It was our joke. He did not need the money, nor could he give legal advice, much less take money for it, according to the terms of his case and probation. My giving him a dollar technically broke the rules and stuck a finger under the nose of the broken legal system. The same system that allowed him to work with criminals to set up legal shell corporations, and then take the fall once discovered. While the criminals, at least so far, had not been arrested.

"Thank you. I'll put this toward my effort to remain disbarred."

"I thought you would have closed the blinds. Since you don't want anyone to know you are associated with me."

"Just the opposite. I assume anyone following you already knows it. The open blinds give them a clear view of you, so they won't shoot me by mistake. Other than a window repair and a new chair to replace the one you are sitting in, I come out ahead."

"I see your point and can't argue with the logic. But aren't you just as likely to be on a hit list as me?"

"Now it is my turn to see your point. I need to invest in steel blinds to deflect any bullets regardless of who is here with me."

"Would not it be hilarious if we both got shot right now, by different people for different reasons?"

"There is some humor there, but I don't share your enthusiasm for what would be painful for both of us."

"True. But even more painful for your cleaning service."

"I doubt it. They would merely be annoyed, but paid to clean it up. While we would be dead. Now, to what do I owe the pleasure of your company today?"

"Larry, in your previous iteration as a lawyer doing dirty

deals, I ran across some papers where you did business with Benjamin Rawley."

"I remember him. A pompous bureaucrat from the Warm Springs campus. He and some others had various crooked deals going, including some on campus."

"That is him. I assume the information you turned over to the authorities was only part of your vast files and knowledge of the multiple criminal enterprises you worked with. Surely you kept some to protect yourself in case they had plans to come after you. Especially since the state ended your protective detail."

"I could not say for sure without incriminating myself."

"Well said. I'll not ask you about anyone or anything except for Benjamin Rawley."

"Do you want the kind of information that can blackmail him, get him fired, or get him killed?"

"That is a conundrum. All three? Just kidding. I think getting him fired is good enough. Although I once thought I had enough on him to make that happen. But somehow he survived."

"His only redeeming characteristic is that he knows a few powerful people at the Statehouse in Atlanta. Otherwise, he would have been gone by now. Back to my question. You need something to get him fired, so who else do you want to be implicated?"

"I would hope no one else. Just Ben."

"That will be tough. All his misdeeds were intertwined with others."

"I see. Can you give me a couple of scenarios, names redacted of course, and let me choose one?"

"I can do that. But the fee is double due to the extra work."

"No problem."

"Give me a few days to pry out the good stuff and arrange it."

"I'm not in a great hurry. Thanks."

I drove home and thought about my life lately. Called to Britain to help an ex-wife out with a murder investigation. Only to get involved in a Russian methamphetamine operation. But I got to know her daughter and made a friend. Then I came home to get dumped by my new girlfriend, Donna, and then get shot at by an unknown assailant. And getting partially bought out of my bookstore. My only anchors were my house, which was a historical cottage, a dilapidated guest cottage out back, and Kat. Those were all good things. With the bookstore mostly gone, I now had time for those things.

I had already signed the papers, and my bank account had perked up from the partial bookstore buyout. The biggest change for me was not working at the bookstore every day. I could take it two days a week. More if Millard or Lottie were gone, less if I needed time elsewhere. Oh, and Lottie had decided to give it a real name. My meager contribution to the initial documents to open it had listed it as the Warm Springs Bookstore. Lottie felt it needed something more marketable, but she had not decided what it might be yet. I'd leave it to her to come up with something catchy.

I thought about Donna, although I did not want to. I would miss our dating relationship, but knew she was right about us not being in the same place. Trying to be friends was interesting and going OK so far. Bryan drove me home from the hospital after the shooting, and Donna was waiting for me. She had brought dinner, and we had a nice time talking. She left afterward but had continued texting to ask about me. We were talking more now than when we dated. I told her about Elizabeth, my ex-wife's daughter, calling me. Donna encouraged me to go over and see Elizabeth when she began studying in Amsterdam. I just might, especially if Olivia, her mother and my ex, would not be there.

For the foreseeable future, though, I'd be investigating my own shooting. More importantly, I'd be home with Kat and working in the garden. Fall harvest was coming up soon, and winter planting was well underway. Other than someone trying to kill me, I really enjoyed being in Warm Springs.

CHAPTER TWO

I reread Bryan's report about my attempted shooting. I had the official report, but my version had a few hand-written notes from him. The location of the shooter was noted, which was the edge of the thin line of woods on the other side of the grass field beside my house. No evidence was recovered there. A few cut twigs to give the shooter a better view of my house was the only disturbance of the scene. Just behind the woods was one of the roads leading to a campus exit. The shooter could have been out of the woods and in a car in thirty seconds. Then off campus in not much more than a minute.

Nobody had noticed a car there nor one leaving campus in a hurry. But there were only trees from there to the exit, so that was not surprising. If the shooter left on foot, bicycle, or motorcycle, they could have even gone through the woods and left campus from multiple places. The undeveloped State Park and Little White House grounds surrounded most of campus, and both had access roads the shooter could have used to flee.

The first bullet was shattered into pieces when it hit the roof rack on my tank of a car. The second one I never heard embedded in a tree on the strip of trees between my house and the police station next door. The report came back that it was a .270 caliber bullet. I had questions about that choice of gun and would be talking to Bryan about it since he was handling the investigation. Beyond that, there was no real evidence other than the gash on my neck caused by roof rack shrapnel.

I also planned to confer with my secret investigative weapon. Millard and his OctoPosse were probably already on the case. But I would go over to his house and make it official. He and a group of his local buddies, including at least one woman, represented hundreds of years of experience and knowledge. They were all once leaders and respected members of their various professions. Now retired, forgotten and looking for a purpose, they had found it in assisting me in investigating crimes. They had their own interests as well, from high-stakes poker games to running a competitive betting pool on who would solve cases and when. I was definitely going to use their help to solve my case.

My third line of inquiry I would keep to myself. I needed a conference with my contact in the Dixie Mafia in Atlanta. He had already warned me something like this was possible, but assured me they would notify me before it happened. Something had slipped by them, or maybe they were telling me something by not telling me. Since we were family, even though I had distanced myself from them, I doubted they would let me get shot on a contract hit without prior warning.

There was no reason to put it off any longer. I began the process to set up the official call. I wondered whether all this was even necessary. The federal agents and the tech industry probably had every phone call monitored regardless of any procedures to circumvent them. I made the call to the payphone, got a burner phone ready, and waited for a return call. Mine burner phone rang, and I answered.

"Hey," I said.

"Hey." Neither of us were great conversationalists.

"Do all these precautions for phone calls even work anymore?"

"We know all calls can now be monitored. But more than 90 percent are not regularly recorded, much less listened to right now. Yet if I called you on my cell and you answered on yours, there is a 100 percent chance it would be recorded and listened to by a human agent. So we play the odds and figure most of these calls are safe. Even so, most everything we discuss is not incriminating."

"Got it."

"We were expecting your call. We heard about your problem, but have not interfered since we knew you were OK. And there has been nothing on our end to rectify."

"What do you mean?"

"It would be highly disadvantageous, probably even incredibly unhealthy, for someone to poach in our territory. I know it seems like a totally different area down there, but it's only an hour from Atlanta and our jurisdiction. I also know it could happen if people were brought in from outside for a special job. But even that information seeps out over time, and there has been nothing leaked since your incident. Which means we have not had to take any action yet."

"I understand. I'm not sure myself it was a professional try. They were careful, but they tried two head shots from a long distance with a .270 caliber rifle."

There was silence on the other end as those facts sank in. "Most unusual. Nobody I know of in our orbit would use that caliber. But I'll check around to see if anybody up north or out west does. I'm sure you know all our guys go for center mass torso for the first two shots. And they would opt for something heavier like a .308."

"Yeah, I figured. Something tells me this was a local amateur. Or a pro trying to look like an amateur."

"True, but the .270 shoots nice and flat. A pro still would not have missed your head twice."

"Anyway, if you hear something, let me know."

"I will. Take care and let me know if you need a guy down there. Don't want this happening again."

"Thanks, but no need to send anyone." But I thought he probably would, anyway. If I saw a stranger around that didn't try to kill me, it would be one of his men.

"Whatever you say. Good luck."

"Oh, something else that might be important."

"Go."

"On my recent trip to the UK, I sort of stumbled into a Russian mob hit connected to an international methamphetamine operation."

There was a long silence. So long that I wondered if the connection had been cut. "Jimmy, this is important. Tell me what happened. Unless you did something not mentionable on the phone. And do they know who you are?"

He sounded serious. And I had not been called Jimmy since I was a teenager. "I was helping out a woman whose husband had been killed. The police were acting as if she were their main suspect. Turns out the dead guy was supplying chemicals to the Russians and their competitors, which was not appreciated. But the police higher-ups knew all along as they were running an operation on the Russians. It is still active. I got tossed out of the country after calling Interpol and asking questions. I think the Russians have a good idea of who I am."

"You really stepped into it. I've got some work to do on this. You be extra careful. How did you get involved?"

"The woman, the wife of the dead man, was Olivia, my first wife."

"The cute British girl?"

"Yeah, that one. She now works for and is protected by the British police."

"I doubt the Russians will do anything since you already came back, but still better to be cautious."

"I will. Thanks for checking."

The next day, it was my turn to work at the bookstore. Millard and Lottie had told me to ignore the schedule because they would cover for me, but I felt I needed to get out and resume my Warm Springs life. With Kat in her carrier on the back of the bike, I pedaled into town. I was a little more wary and aware of my surroundings, but it was only a five-minute ride. The only thing I noticed was a motorcycle pulling out of campus behind me when I turned onto the main road. It stayed back and never got close to me, although the speed limit was 35 mph. It was not a threat, so I forgot about it.

Kat and I opened the store and began our day. She circled the store, sniffing and rubbing her head along the shelves at the usual spots, then jumped up on my desk to lick herself for a few minutes. Her hair was not out of place, but she felt the need to tidy up after the breezy ride. I looked through some paperwork, but there was nothing to do as Lottie, one of my new partners, already had inventory, taxes, and orders for the next two weeks handled.

I decided to relieve my boredom by doing some writing. My muse was on break, so after a few minutes I took a new bestseller off the shelf to begin reading. I did not get far as I realized once again how much slop the big publishers pushed onto the public. The marketing of big names now replaced anything resembling good writing. Between ghostwriters and AI, I also had to wonder how much good new material was coming along through the big publishing houses. Regardless, the book in my hand was not worth the time investment required. I put it back and looked up the sales record for the store. Thirteen copies were sold in ten days. People were actually buying it. Yet I could not recommend it and, for the first time, realized maybe I should not be in the book business.

I toughed it out until lunch and went next door to Mable's Diner. I did not see Lottie. With the lunch crowd coming in, I sat at the bar to keep a table open. The special was a hot bowl of goodness, all local. Greens, beans, onions, peppers, and tomatoes. It was served on rice, which I doubted was local, but I ate it anyway. I ordered it with roast chicken on the side. Instead of eating it, I'd take it back to

Kat for her lunch. If I kept in her good graces, maybe she would take me with her when the mothership landed and took all the cats to another galaxy. It sounded like a bad late-night science fiction movie and had probably been filmed. But she would get fed just in case.

Back at the store, I fed Kat. She ate and jumped in the window to lick herself and take another nap. The afternoon dragged, but there were a few customers. Another copy of the bad new bestseller went out. I desperately wanted to tell them it was not good, but it was not my place. Everyone had different criteria for choosing and reading a particular book. It was a personal choice and something I should not interfere with. I decided I could recommend other books, better books, to those customers once they finished the bestseller.

Mid-afternoon, Lottie came over to relieve me and watch Kat while I went for a doctor's appointment. I had not been stitched up the night after the shooting to let the wound drain. But before going home the next day, Dr. Hoffman put in three stitches to keep my brains from falling out of my neck. Those were her words, not mine. It was time to have them removed. Apparently, the skin was intact enough to prevent brain spillage.

As I got on my bike, I thought I saw a motorcycle parked across the street in a shady alley between buildings. I don't know why I noticed it as there were usually multiple motor-cycles in Warm Springs on any day. A remnant from the time when the town was marketed as a biker destination. I'm sure it seemed like a good marketing idea at the time. Quiet motorbikes, driven by wealthy Atlantans, mostly doctors and dentists, coming down to spend money. Of course, the motorcycle crowd was composed of a much larger swath of demographics than the one envisioned by the former town leaders. Loud bikes ridden by those looking for a raucous, drunken trip had convinced the town to look for other advertising measures.

There was no rider in sight near the motorcycle, so I hopped on my bike and pedaled back toward campus. Not even a minute later, I turned left on the edge of town for the hospital.

CHAPTER THREE

I was seeing Dr. Hoffman at the hospital as she did not have a private office in town. One part of the hospital was set up for the local doctors to provide outpatient services, so that is where I went. It was a slow day for medicine in Hamilton County, so I did not have to wait.

"Ah, my favorite patient," she said.

"What a coincidence; you are my favorite doctor."

"Then I'm your only one."

"There is that."

"Let me check your neck. Any swelling, redness, or unusual pain?"

"Are you asking me if I am a pain in the neck?"

"That is the one question I don't need to ask."

"Anyway, nothing abnormal with the wound. You must

have gotten everything out and cleaned with no obvious infectious processes."

"Excellent. I will apply some alcohol and snip out these three stitches. You may feel a little pinch."

"Do your worst."

"My oath won't allow me to follow my instincts. Hold still, please." I felt the coldness of the alcohol swab, then a few tiny twinges as the stitch was pulled through the skin. Then I heard a noise.

"Oh, I may have to finish this up and leave," she said.

"Is it a hospital emergency where you need to rush off and save someone?"

"Not exactly. This text refers to someone already deceased."

"I don't get it. Unless you are a lot worse doctor than I thought."

"Somehow I have ended up being the backup for the county coroner. If a body is found, I get a call or text alert. The coroner takes the case, but I can accompany if I'm available. Part of the training."

"I just want you to know I had nothing to do with this body. I guess if my shooter had been better, you and I would have met in different circumstances."

"Regarding the new body, it is too early to plead innocence. If it were foul play, you could still be a suspect."

"Only if the person was run over by a bicycle. But I would probably remember that."

"And here is the confirmation text from the coroner. You were my last appointment for the afternoon, and the hospital is quiet. I need to leave and take care of this."

"Go ahead, doc. I think I'll survive now that the three

stitches are out. Meanwhile, I should not do anything too stupid or strenuous and keep an eye out for any redness or swelling in the next few days."

"Exactly. You've done this before. Now excuse me, I need to get my kit and leave."

"Knock 'em dead, doc." Ouch, that was bad even for me.

She did not say anything but held her nose as she walked out. I got the message.

I left the hospital and went back to the bookstore to grab Kat and go home. Lottie would keep the store the next hour and a half before closing. I think it worked in her favor as she did not have to close up Mable's. Someone else would get that privilege while Lottie hung out in the comfortable, air-conditioned store.

My ride home was uneventful. No motorcycles anywhere. I was getting paranoid. But that reminded me to get my small pistol and begin carrying it when I left the house. Although I'd probably forget it most days. Kat hit the yard to do her chipmunk and rodent rounds. I pulled some food out of the refrigerator from my meal prep day on Saturday. A mix of grilled vegetables, roast chicken, and cut fruit.

This week I added some late-season blueberries to the apples and pears. There would not be any more fresh blue-berries for the year, but I had plenty in the freezer. The berries were tiny but very flavorful and had a little kick. Excellent in my fruit salad.

The blueberries were brought from Maine and given to me by Sam and Irene. They were Emma's cousins and lived nearby. Their business took them to Maine twice a year to pick up inventory, and this time I also got berries.

Kat came to the door because she knew it was dinner-time. I put chicken in her bowl, and we proceeded to eat. She finished first as usual and kindly waited for me to finish as she sat in the foyer and groomed her face. I got up and let her out to finish the last of the daylight outside. Because of all the wildlife on the ten thousand acres around campus, she was not allowed outside after dark.

As the sun neared the horizon, and the heat broke for the day, I went to the front porch. Bryan came around the thick growth of trees and vines that separated my yard from that of the police station.

"How is that cat of yours doing?" he asked. He stopped and watched her crouch down and then start a belly walk. She was stalking a grasshopper. They were large this time of year and made worthy adversaries. But unless it flew off before she pounced on it, I was betting on her.

"Depends on whether she conquers the grasshopper. If she loses, I'll have to dry her tears and give her a snack as consolation."

"Cat people are weird."

"Cats say the same about humans."

"You just made my point."

"Insolence, intolerable human. I am going to have some iced tea. Want some?"

"Sure."

Inside, I poured ice and tea into two tall glasses and brought them out to the porch. Bryan took a long sip as we took a moment to listen to the early katydids.

"How's the neck?" Bryan asked.

"It is fine now since it has been de-stitched. Although it

was a near thing, as Doc Hoffman had to run out on me to attend a dead body."

"Oh, so you've heard then."

"I don't think so. She took out the stitches, answered a text and said she had to go. I pedaled home for dinner."

"What do you think about Doctor Hoffman?"

"I think she is intelligent, well-educated, and attractive in a doctorly fashion. Why do you ask?"

"She is new in town, and you are single, so…"

"No. No, not going to happen. She is ten years, maybe even fifteen years younger than me. She is busy at the hospital and chasing dead bodies with the coroner. But in case you did not hear me, I said no."

"A lot of denial words when you could have just said you weren't interested."

"Whatever. But I think you are trying to distract me from asking about the body."

"I was. Not that it matters much since I don't know a lot yet. Other than it was found in a provocative manner. Luckily, it's out of my jurisdiction, so the interim sheriff gets the honors. No late nights for me with this one."

"OK, now you have to tell me the provocative part and where it was found."

"You ever been to the Cove?"

"Oh yes."

"The body was placed in the dish of one of the large radio astronomy antenna arrays. The ones used for some kind of communication signals some time ago. Still in Hamilton County, so the new interim sheriff, poor guy, gets the case."

"You are telling me somebody put a body up there? Are

you sure it was not somebody drunk who climbed up on it and expired?"

"That is what I thought too. But it looks like a homicide. Not sure whether he was killed there or later placed on the antenna. Either way, that took a lot of effort."

"Those things are huge and high off the ground."

"Yes, they are a hundred feet in diameter. The lowest portion of the dish is almost thirty feet above the ground."

"A winch was used then. Or a catapult, but that would have been messy."

"Apparently, it was messy anyway. Lot of blood on the white dish. That is what got someone's attention as they drove past. I heard a deputy on the radio say something about a word being spelled out, but the interim sheriff hushed him up."

"At least neither of us is involved this time. I just want a nice, quiet fall. I'm waiting for the first frost to kill off the poison ivy and knock down the ticks so I can hike the woods trails."

"I know what you mean. I want to eat dinner with the family, watch the kids play fall baseball, and go to high school football games."

"Here's to a quiet and relaxing fall," I said, holding up my glass.

"I'll drink to that," Bryan said, raising his glass and clinking it against mine. "Except of course, the one open case of attempted murder I have on my caseload."

"Oh that. I almost forget it most days. It just seems unimportant somehow."

"You seem nonchalant considering someone tried to blow your head off with a rifle."

"Yes, but the little I know makes me think it was an amateurish, onetime thing. And the list of suspects is so long I don't know how to even begin sifting it down."

"You don't feel threatened? Maybe that is how they want you to feel, so next time they will get closer and won't need a rifle."

"Maybe. But inexplicably, I am not registering a threat."

"Any idea why?"

"A few things. The attempt to shoot at my head for one thing. I doubt a pro would do that. Especially at that distance of nearly 200 yards."

"Did you check with your Atlanta people?"

"Yes, and they said the same thing. And before you ask, they confirmed there was no official contract out on me."

"OK, what else?"

"The rifle caliber. None of the pros use a .270 caliber rifle."

"I had the same thought. Plus, most all those guns are bolt actions. Because of the delay to reload another bullet, the shooter better get it right on the first shot."

"You heard the second shot, but I did not. Was there a delay?

"There was. Two to three seconds. About what you'd expect for a person on a bolt action. It takes time to slide the action back, slide it forward, then get back in the scope."

"A bolt action .270 is a popular rifle for deer hunting around here, isn't it?"

"Definitely. Especially where there are clear sight lines and no brush."

"That is why I think it is a local. And they may not try

again. But I can't live everyday worrying about one of my neighbors shooting me at close range or stabbing me."

"True, but you have a list, even if it is a long one. With some help, you could at least narrow it down. Find out if some were out of town that day or at work, for example. You might have 50 people, but I bet we could get it down to 20."

"That makes sense. I can give you a list, and the same one goes to the OctoPosse."

"The what?"

"Millard's group."

"Good idea. They can get information that I can't. Thanks for the tea, I have to go home."

"Thanks Bryan. I'll email you the list."

I dropped by Millard's to give him the same list. He was on the porch and wearing a deep blue vest, or waistcoat, with yellow seahorses. I had not seen that one before.

"Hi Millard, feeling like visiting an aquarium today?"

"Oh, that is funny coming from a guy posing as a paper target."

"True enough. But the awful thing is they broke my roof rack. Getting that fixed is worse than a hospital bill."

"Don't worry about it. Roof racks are cheaper than brains. Those are scarce these days."

"Yeah, and I would like to keep what I have."

"What can I do for you today?"

"I brought a list of people who might want to do me harm. I was hoping your group could take a look at it. Maybe narrow it down if you knew any that were out of town, at work at the time, that kind of thing. Fair warning, some are names of people, others are occupations because I don't know what the names are for the local owners or operators."

"Explain that one."

"I know there are some tree cutters around here, so I listed them by profession. I did so because Benjamin Rawley was working on a deal to get the campus trees clear cut. When I quashed the deal, I assume at least one of the local tree cutters lost some lucrative business."

"OK, makes some sense. Let me take a look at your list. Yeah, OK, missed one, missed another; yep a definite possibility."

"Have you already seen the list somehow?"

"Way ahead of you. We put ours together the evening after the shooting. Been whittling it down since. I think we have most of yours already covered, but I'll go over it again. We'll add any we need to and keep working it."

"Thanks Millard."

"Hey, you keep giving us something to do."

"Oh, I came up with a name for your group I've been using. Thought I would tell you in case you didn't like it."

"Let's hear it, smart guy."

"Octoposse."

Millard cocked his head. Looked up to the left, then down to the right. I got the impression he was rolling a marble around inside his head, trying to get it to fall into place.

"Not the worst thing I've ever heard. I'll submit it to the group, and we'll have a vote."

"Really, just like that?"

"No, of course not. I'll think about it. I'll use it to prod the others to adopt it or come up with something better. They probably won't, though. I'll bring it up during poker night. Might distract them enough so I can win a few hands."

"Thanks and good luck."

CHAPTER FOUR

Sam and Irene lived in the Cove. It was capitalized because it is a real place name. Just outside the small town of Woodbury, the Cove was actually a crater. Whether an impact crater or some other geological anomaly, it was still up for debate. But a round crater three or four miles across with a flat bottom surrounded by a circular ridge a few hundred feet tall seemed to me to fit an impact site.

Sam and Irene were cousins of my late wife, Emma. I had reached out to them a year ago and now we had lunch regularly and kept up with life. Emma also came over to walk on campus occasionally. They had helped me with a recent case on Hamilton County's marijuana operations. They no longer took part in those ventures, but ran a business in another grey area.

Sam and Irene obtained and transported marijuana

edibles, supplying them in the local region. It was mostly legal except that some of the states they transported across considered the practice illegal. Their recent trip to Maine that resulted in my blueberry windfall was to get their product, the edibles. Pulling a camper and acting as law-abiding tourists, the states between Georgia and Maine would likely never even know that edibles crossed their lines. Even so, states like Pennsylvania and North Carolina required care when they traveled, and they avoided South Carolina completely. Even Georgia had varying laws regarding edibles, and every state could change laws from year to year. More confusing was that some edibles were legal while others were not.

I got a call from Sam the next morning. It was not my day at the bookstore so I was still home.

"Hi, Sam how is it going?"

"Doing Ok, I guess. How is your situation?"

"Not bad, other than someone trying to shoot me. But I've decided it won't happen again so I'm not panicking. I'll eventually get around to finding who did it, or someone else will."

"That is a very lenient philosophy."

"I guess, but based more on practicality than leniency. Whoever did it should still get spanked by the law when they finally surface. I heard you had some excitement over in your neighborhood the past day or two."

"Well, yes, we did. On that subject, I'm wondering if you have time to come over."

"I'm not doing anything today. How about in a half hour or so?"

"That would be great. We'll be waiting on you at the house."

"See you then."

That was odd. My red flag sense told me something was going on. I had a sneaking suspicion they had heard something about the body and wanted to talk about it. I had been around for a couple of investigations, mostly unofficially, but I guess people were associating me with working on criminal investigations. Funny, because two years ago I never would have thought I'd be doing this. But life's currents and eddies can take you to some interesting places.

I left Kat inside since I did not know how long I'd be gone. As I got in my tank of a car I once again saw the roof rack, damaged on one side by the bullet that missed my head. I had no idea how much an old Land cruiser rack cost, but imagined I was about to get sticker shock when I got around to replacing it. Better that than replacing my skull.

The Cove was about a fifteen to twenty-minute drive, depending on the route. I went the long way through Woodbury. It was an old Southern town that had been up and down more than once. In the town itself were a number of older large building once serving as warehouses or sheds. Some were nothing more than piles of crumbling bricks and fallen roofs. Others had been remodeled and now housed antique markets along the main street.

When I first came to the area, I didn't know the history. A large mural painted on a surviving wall proclaimed Woodbury the "pimento capital of the world." I had not seen any large expanses of pepper plants around the town, although it was an agricultural area. But what I saw were hay fields, pine plantations, and peach orchards. Later I found out that farmers in the general area were looking for alternatives after cotton's demise. The boll weevil, changing labor markets, and international competitors made cotton untenable. Some farmers began growing pimentos which caught on. Woodbury became a massive global supplier, with packing sheds and processing plants in town. Some of the very buildings now crumbling or transformed into antique stores were part of the pimento wave.

All good things go bad. Pimentos only have value to consumers when the skin is removed. That required a large, unskilled and underpaid work force used to manually peel the peppers. Woodbury had plenty of people, but pepper companies knew there were entire countries full of cheap labor overseas. By the early 1980s the companies were gone from the US, and Woodbury once again slumped.

Later, in an odd turn of events, a wildly popular television series came to town. People could get hired as extras, and the show put Woodbury on the map again. All you had to do was dress up as a zombie and lurch around, slowly chasing the buffet of human characters on the show. Of course, that went away as well. Now Woodbury was in the early stages of gentrification, drawing a few Atlantans and others from New York and California with low prices, nice homes, and a quiet life.

I passed through and turned right toward the Cove. The rolling land soon rose to a higher, steeper ridge on the left. I turned in that direction on Cove Road, the in-and-out two-lane that serviced the crater. I was coming in from the north end, and Sam and Irene lived on the south ridge. The road took me to the antenna array impossible to miss along the way. Two white dish antennas, a hundred feet in diameter, suspended off the ground by short squat towers of girders and engines designed to move the huge dishes. A couple of outbuildings were encircled by a tall chain-link fence with a locked gate.

As it appeared on my right, I could see the area marked off with yellow police tape. The dish nearest the road also had a large green tarp fastened across part of the bottom of the dish. The lowest part of the lip was still thirty feet up. That tarp must have been where the body was found. As I continued driving, I thought it was an unusual placement for a murdered body. The killer was posing the body for anyone driving on the road to see. Proud of his work or sending a message? That would be somebody else's job to decipher.

The mostly flat bottom of the crater I drove along was a few open fields and lots of trees. Not many houses, but a few nice barns, including a beautiful old red barn. A few minutes later I pulled into Sam and Irene's driveway. It twisted up the steep ridge through the trees to their house near the top. I applauded their decision to leave all trees possible, although I'm sure it was not easy to build the road or haul up building supplies.

Sam and Irene were outside and waiting for me at the top by the house. As I got out, I took a moment to look at the view. It would be much better once the leaves fell, but I could still see a glint of the Flint River down below.

"Hi folks, how are you both doing?" I asked.

"We are good," Sam said.

"How are you doing?" Irene asked.

"I am fine, just staying away from people with deer rifles."

"I can understand that. Any closer to finding out who did it?"

"No, not really. But I'm not worried. I figured it was a onetime thing from a local, and probably won't happen again."

"I hope not," Sam said. "They might get lucky next time."

"Possibly. What did you want to talk about?"

They did not say anything as they looked at each other. Finally Sam spoke up.

"We need your advice about something. Maybe some help if you are willing to give it."

"I will do what I can. Although I might not bury the body for you." It was supposed to be a joke but neither of them cracked a smile. Something serious was happening.

"Maybe I need to show you something," Sam said. "Irene, you should stay here."

"I'd be happy to," she said.

We got in Sam's truck and went down the hill. He was unusually quiet on the way. At the bottom of the drive, he turned left and went a short distance before turning left into a field. It was a level hayfield, and I could tell it sloped slightly down to the Flint River, masked by a line of trees. Just before the trees was a nice red barn. It was about as picturesque as a rural area in Georgia could be. Sam stopped in front of the barn. I followed him inside after he removed the padlock from the large rolling door. He quickly closed it behind us.

The dim interior showed the floor was dirt in the four stalls along one side of a large open area. Where we stood it was concrete. There was a folding table along one planked wall, with a coffeemaker and microwave, indicating the barn had electricity and water connection.

In the middle of the concrete before us in the dim light

was a nice old stepside pickup truck. A late 1950s Ford as best as I could tell, and I only knew that because my grandfather had owned a similar one many years in the past.

"Sam, I didn't know you collected antique trucks," I said, as I reached to put my hand on the tailgate.

"Stop! I would not do that if I were you," Sam said. I froze, my hand in midair. "Sorry for yelling, but you need to look this thing over without touching it. Take a peek in the bed first."

I put my hand down and looked in. The bed, small compared to current trucks, appeared to be poorly painted a dark red. But the smell attested that it was not paint, but rather old blood.

"I'm going to assume that this is not your truck," I said. "Also, this is not your blood, or you'd be dead. Therefore, either somebody dressed a deer in here, or this truck is tied to that body found on the big antenna dish."

"The latter is the correct answer."

"That brings up a lot of questions."

"I know, but I don't have many answers."

"Let's start by how this truck got into this barn."

"I can answer that. The other night the driveway sensor went off. Probably about 3 am. If someone pulls in or leaves it dings once. This time it just kept going. Woke us up as we had not had that happen since a delivery truck parked in the drive one afternoon. I got my gun and went down to see what was happening."

"And?"

"This truck was sitting there, the engine still running. Nobody was around so I reached in and turned it off. Yelled out a few times but no answer from anyone. I was not sure what to do with it, but did not want to leave it in the driveway. I got in to drive it over to the side of the road. Once inside, I figured I should see who it belonged to. I opened the dash box to grab the registration. That's when I knew something was wrong."

"Got it so far. I'm guessing you knew the owner."

"Too well for a time. Then not at all as our paths diverged."

"Then you drove it here to the barn."

"Yeah, after I saw the registration, I glanced back and looked in the bed. The moon was out and I could see it was shiny back there. Turned on the flashlight and about had a heart attack. Decided the truck needed to be somewhere besides the front of my house. But now my fingerprints were on it, so I brought it over here to wipe it down. Even though I was shook up I had enough sense to check for tracking devices. Found one under the wheel well so I disabled it."

"How did you disable it?"

"Put it in the microwave for ten seconds. It arced and went crispy."

"Is this your barn?"

"Technically, no. Through one of our companies, we hold a lease for the field and barn. The barn gives us additional storage although we have not had to use it yet."

"And another place to hide the camper you transport product with, if you need it."

"Exactly."

"Can the truck be tracked here?"

"I don't think so. I found and disabled the tracker quick enough. It is not that far from the driveway. The tracker may not have even shown the truck was moved before it quit transmitting. I think it is safe here, at least for now."

"So who does it belong to?"

"Lester Owens. A descendant of one of the old farming families from Woodbury."

"I don't know the name. But the truck looks familiar. I think I noticed it in Woodbury a couple of times. My grandfather had a similar one, but not in this good of shape."

"You probably saw it there. He did not drive it much except for parades, but sometimes on a Sunday he'd take it to town."

"Is it he who was found dead in the dish?"

"The police have not made an official announcement, but the rumors in town say it was Lester."

"That would have made it hard for him to have driven the truck to your driveway."

"Especially after having lost all that blood. If Lester was murdered, the killer left his truck in my driveway."

"There aren't many assisted suicides around here so I'm betting on murder. But the way the body was left in the dish tells me it was meant to be seen."

"And the truck was meant to be seen in my driveway. If not for the sensor going off, half a dozen people and the sheriff would have seen it the next morning. Irene and I would have been in the police station getting asked lots of questions."

"Do you want to go back to the house and figure out what to do next?"

"Yeah, this blood is not getting any fresher, and soon the flies will be on it."

CHAPTER FIVE

We did not talk on the short ride back to the house. Inside, Sam sat at the kitchen as Irene came in.

"James, can I get you some coffee?" she asked.

"That would be great, Irene."

"You saw what was in the barn?"

"Yes."

"What do you think about it?"

"So far, I'd say somebody really did not like Lester, and you guys are on the same list."

"That's what we think."

"How did you guys know Lester?"

Sam and Irene looked at each other before replying. I was sure that they had already had that conversation and were working out how much they wanted to tell me. I hoped it was the truth because they had been implicated in a murder, and now they were hiding evidence.

"We worked with him a long time ago," Sam said. "In a different business than we are now in, and much more illegal. Lester at the time was an up-and-comer at the local Savings and Loan. He was on target to be the next president and needed cash influxes to prove his worth to the organization."

"He laundered your money?"

"Yes. Back then it was easier to hide it. Besides, it wasn't like the cocaine business where you needed to hide a million dollars a week. Lester was taking $30 to $40 thousand a week from us. We got back $25 thousand, which was held in the S&L account. Lester kept the difference for himself, plus the large account made him look good."

"How did it end? Based on what you said I'm assuming you have not done business in a while."

"We got out of what we were doing. Too risky. We wanted to take all the money out of the S&L but Lester threatened us."

"I don't see how that would work. He would have implicated himself."

"It wasn't the police he was threatening us with. He said he would tell our former competitors who we were and where we lived."

"What did you do?

"Nothing at first. We needed to make plans. Get the money and change our identities, then find a new town to live in."

"Then the bottom fell out," Irene said. "It no longer mattered."

"What do you mean?"

"Lester was running the S&L by then," she continued. "He had overextended on shady mortgages and a number of unsecured loans. Some federal government agency shut them down, I think in 1990 or so."

"Did the money disappear?"

"All of it. Luckily we had always kept some cash each week and put it away. We always thought the feds would find out and confiscate the S&L money. We never considered Lester would double-cross us and then get the S&L into trouble."

"You have not been in contact since then?"

"No, we had no reason to," Sam said. "Even if things had gone differently, we would have parted ways."

"If we saw him out somewhere we ignored each other," Irene said.

"Somebody had to have known you once did business," I said. "Otherwise leaving the truck in your driveway was pure coincidence."

"We don't believe it was."

"I don't either."

"If you were in our place, what would you do?"

"Honestly I'd be torn between calling the sheriff and wiping the truck down and driving it into a deep pond to never be seen again."

"That is what we have been talking about. Right now we have decided to do nothing with the truck, while trying to figure out who might be behind it."

"Makes sense to me. If the truck can be tied back to the murderer it could just reappear somewhere in the woods, without your prints. But tell me, what would you like me to do?"

"Think about what we should do about the truck. If possible, help us find the killer," Sam said.

"But we know you have other concerns, like finding the person who shot at you," Irene said.

"Maybe we will get really lucky and it will be the same person," I said.

"Doubtful."

"Did Lester have other vehicles besides the old truck?"

"Yeah, he had several. He normally drove an older Cadillac. Why?"

"Seems like the killer was sending a message by displaying the body in the dish. Would have been a lot simpler just disappearing the body and the killer would have been much less likely to get caught. There was another message sent by leaving the vehicle in your driveway. I'm betting there was also a message the killer was sending by choosing that particular truck. Solve those three riddles and find the killer."

"Sounds easy."

"It never is. But maybe we will get lucky. That has always worked for me."

As soon as I got in the car to thread down the steep and winding driveway, I began thinking. Lester once laundered money from illegal activities through his bank. If he was doing it for Sam and Irene, I wondered who else might have been using him. He got cute and tried to make even more money, then got the S&L busted out. Other crooks getting money laundered, plus regular people losing their savings must have made Lester a long list of enemies. But at least one person wanting him dead knew about his former relation-ship with Sam and Irene. There probably were not that many people in the county that knew that connection. This was a problem that Bryan could not help me with, nor the interim sheriff. My most useful sources of information were off limits this time. But if I could determine the proper way to present it, I was betting the Octoposse could take on the challenge.

As I drove out I noticed a disheveled gentleman pushing a shiny shopping cart down the side of the road. He wore old but clean clothes and boots, but a dirty baseball cap. He stared as I went past but I did not know him. Not unusual in urban areas but I had not seen something like that outside of Manchester in Hamilton County. The Cove was a few miles from Manchester, and even from the nearest grocery store in Woodbury. I filed it away under the category of odd sights and soon had reason to forget about it.

Near the end of Cove Road where I had to turn right, I saw a motorcycle in my rearview mirror behind me coming out of the Cove. Could it have been the one I saw before coming out of campus? I honestly could not remember since it did not seem important at the time. Just in case I took a longer look and tried to commit the cycle to memory. By the time I got to the last turn for the main road I lost it and did not see it again on the way home.

I finished my sandwich and tea on the front porch as Kat lounged on the front walk. She was lazy in the hot weather and had to be yearning for the heat to break. It should be soon, but at the moment we were both acting like turtles and trying not to move much. A car came up the side road and turned onto the road fronting the house. Nothing unusual as a few cars a day did the same on their way to the Georgia Hall or the police station next door. But then the car pulled in my drive. I edged a little closer to the porch railing where my pistol was lying under a newspaper. A paper that I had no intention of reading but did cover the gun nicely. I could see a driver but nothing else. The door opened, and she stood looking at me, almost as if afraid to approach. I was more than a little surprised. I stood and welcomed her.

"Vicky Vickers, how are you doing?"

"James, is it OK if I come to visit?"

"Sure. Come on to the porch."

She had something in her hand that looked familiar. I also noticed just how attractive she was. Even though Doyle, her two-time husband, now dead, had roughed her edges, she must have been the county beauty when younger. Maybe I was noticing her more than our last and only previous meeting because she was dressed nicer. A very complimentary sundress and short heels.

"I heard about what happened," she said walking to the porch. "I know it's a Southern thing about bringing food. So I brought you my bourbon chocolate pecan pie." She handed it to me. The first waft of nice perfume hit me.

"That sounds wonderful."

"I hope so. People tell me it's the best in the county."

"I'm betting it is. Thank you very much. But I'm really not deserving, since I'm not sick or dead yet."

"Still, I wanted you to have it." She leaned down to pet Kat, who was appreciative of the attention. I got another waft of perfume and nearly a view that I knew better than to be caught staring at. I quickly found her car very interesting to view instead.

"Would you like to come in or have some tea?"

"No, I'm on the way somewhere. I have to get going. I just wanted to see you and make sure you were alright."

"And bring me pie."

"Yes, to keep you fed."

"Well, I do appreciate it. I look forward to eating it. How are you doing?"

"Um, I'm OK. I really have to go. Please enjoy the pie."

"Thanks again."

She smiled and got back in her car. I waved as she drove off.

Had I not been to Sam and Irene's earlier, Vicky's visit would have been the oddest thing to have happened in a long while. I had no idea what the visit was really about, but I intended to enjoy the pie.

I took it inside and began to wonder what was going on. Then I ate a slice and didn't care why she brought it, just that she had and it was delicious. I would wonder about the why later. I did notice the pie was in a nice ceramic dish. One that would need to be returned. That would give me the opportunity to ask her what was wrong. Whatever was going on, she wasn't bringing me pie just because someone shot at me.

I saw Bryan coming around the brush from the police station next door.

"Just in time for tea," I said. "You want yours shaken, not stirred?"

"It is too early for James Bond quotes."

"Probably. Want some pie to go with it?"

"Sure. Trish is off with the boys this afternoon, so dinner will be late."

"Not if you go home and cook it."

"That would ensure they would not come back. I have a hard time with toast and ice cubes."

"You should spend some time with Julia Childs."

"Who is that?"

"Never mind. Here is your pie."

"Wow, that is good."

"Courtesy of the widow Vickers."

"Was that her I just saw leaving?"

"The same."

"That is interesting. Possibly alarming."

"I prefer to say strange. The second time I've ever seen her, and she delivers pie."

"Not my business, but it would be safer if that was all that was delivered."

"My thoughts exactly."

"Good thing it is not quite deer season yet. She might have brought venison. I know how much you hate that."

"I really dislike it. Is she a deer hunter?"

"She is, or was. Used to hold the record for the biggest buck shot in Hamilton County a few years ago."

"I'm surprised she didn't shoot Doyle."

"She probably would have if the sheriff hadn't done it first."

"To change the subject, any leads on my shooter?"

"That is what I came over for. Not a peep from anyone. It has been quiet. If it was local, it had to be someone acting alone."

"Sounds about right. To change subjects again, heard anything about the body on the dish?"

"Also very quiet. But the sheriff confirmed the identity.

The deceased was Lester Owens, a long-time resident of Woodbury." I acted as if I'd never heard the name.

"Any cause of death or unusual circumstances, other than the obvious where he was displayed on a massive dish?"

"Nothing so far. The sheriff is keeping details secret. He asked the state for help. The rumor is still going around among the deputies is there was a message written in blood. But again, I don't know what it was."

"Not a very discreet killer. Should make them easier to catch."

"Or they are so smart they will never get caught."

"How many showy murderers do you know that have not been caught?"

"None in this state. Maybe a couple out West."

"Doesn't make sense."

"Murder rarely does. There is always an alternative. But I guess some can't see it, or they just want to do it."

CHAPTER SIX

I had another slice of pie for breakfast with my coffee. Normally an attractive single woman bringing me pie would lead me to believe I was being made an object of affection. But because she was Doyle Vickers' widow, I knew better. Doyle was someone I had once been investigating for the murder of Mike Vickers, his cousin. Before I could pin it on him, the sheriff had his deputies shoot Doyle dead. That was because they were involved in a marijuana operation and were double-crossing each other. Vicky had talked to me before that happened and given me some important information as she was divorcing Doyle a second time. I think she did it to try to get an angle to pry more from Doyle if possible. The former events and Vicky's role told me the unsolicited pie meant something else was going on. Or maybe I was overthinking everything and the widow Vickers really was courting me.

Then the third unusual thing happened. Three things in 24 hours was a record for me. A car pulled up in front of the house. This one I knew, but it was no less surprising. Donna got out and came to the door just as I opened it.

"James, how are you?"

"I'm good, Donna. How about you?"

"I'm fine. I came to check on you."

"Come in. Would you like some pie and coffee?"

"That would be great."

I made her a coffee and gave her a slice of pie. She took a bite and closed her eyes in appreciation.

"This is wonderful James. You really know how to bake."

"Nope, not mine."

"Really? Where did you get it?"

"Vicky Vickers came by last night and gave it to me."

Donna's face tightened, and she stared at me. I felt death in her eyes. I knew she was a great athlete and competitor, but I had never seen this side of her.

"Oh. Why did that... woman... bring you pie?"

"I have no idea whatsoever. Very strange. But I intend to find out when I take the pie dish back to her."

Donna put her fork down. "Are you sure you want to do that? You can give it to me and I'll drop it by her house."

"You know her?"

"We... once crossed paths. After her first divorce, she dated my ex-husband a few times. Maybe even before we got divorced."

"Oh, I had no idea. In that case you cannot take her dish back. Don't want you cracking it over her head. Besides, I smell a rat. Maybe even something to do with Mike Vickers' murder."

"I thought that was solved, and the case closed."

"It was, and still is. But I found something new. Somebody was with Doyle the night he killed Mike. Nobody knows about it but Bryan."

"Do you think it was her?"

"No, I don't. But I bet she might know who it was."

"That does not explain the pie."

"No it does not, and that is what bothers me. Warm Springs has some more secrets."

"James, I know I ended things between us. I'm trying not to be jealous. Nor do I have the right to intrude in your life. But I still care about you. Please don't get involved with Vicky."

"I really appreciate that, Donna. But believe me when I say there will be no hanky panky going on between me and Vicky."

"Hanky panky? Who even says that anymore?"

"Me, apparently. Aren't you glad you dumped me now?"

"I want to be mad at you. And I would like to drop that dish on Vicky's head. But I won't do either. I know you well enough that you won't fall for Vicky's charms like most of the men in the county."

"You are right. I intend to dump her after no more than three dates."

"Oh, you try me James, you try me."

"I know. Now let's talk about something else."

"I came to ask if your neck was OK. And if you have any idea who shot at you."

"The neck is fine. I don't know yet, but I'm hoping

between Bryan and Millard's gang, somebody will ferret out the culprit."

"Is Millard's gang the ones you call Octoposse?"

"The very same. Millard did not seem to mind the name."

"Are you worried the shooter will try again?"

"Not so much. I've gone over everything with Bryan and others. I think it was someone local. They missed and won't shoot at me again. Maybe they will try a car accident or something. But I'm not expecting another shooting."

"Then you won't be biking into Warm Springs with Kat anytime soon."

"That's right. We will take a break. No reason to make it easy for them to run me over. Kat would not be happy."

"Nor would Vicky if it happened before she got her dish back."

"Ouch. I'd rather think she would be devastated if the county's most eligible bachelor went kaput."

"Whoever that bachelor might be, I'm sure she would get over it. Meanwhile you have ruined my taste for this wonderful pie."

"Oh well, more for me."

"I'm leaving now. I am glad you are OK. Thanks for the coffee."

"Thanks for checking on me."

After Donna left, I wondered if there was any jealousy lingering there, or if it was more anger that Vicky had dated her ex. Neither was my concern, so I dumped another batch of information in the "to be forgotten" bin in my mind. I needed to get to the garden and meet the group for another harvest and do some preparation for cold weather plantings. Each year it seemed the warm weather persisted slightly longer than the previous year. Which was good for the cold crops but kept the pesky insects around a little later than they should be.

Ernie and Wes, George, Edna were already at the garden. Robert dropped Alisha off. He was keeping Alice so we would not get to see her today. I noticed Robert was driving a large black pickup. Ison said he might come, but had cancelled because his wife's mother had gone into hospice.

I remembered who was almost surely buried under our patch of garden. It was urgent I get to the archives to figure out more details of what happened back in the 1940s, and who wrote the letter detailing the three murders. But between getting shot at and agreeing to help Sam and Irene, the eighty-year-old mystery would need to wait a little longer. I was working on a plan to get rid of any remains under the garden, but that would have to wait until winter.

Meanwhile, us gardeners had to keep the newly planted peas watered in the heat as they sprouted and grew. There should be a nice crop of them after the weather turned cool. Peas were good to eat and helped the soil, fixing nitrogen in the soil for future crops. Fall pea planting normally was not done in Georgia so this was an experiment. Keeping the plants alive in the late heat in the hopes of extended cool weather before winter set in was a bet that the changed weather might make it work. Worst case, we had lost five dollars worth of seed and made the soil a little better.

The pumpkins were coming along well, along with some specialty squash that would make nice decorations. I suppose they were edible, but I'd never prepared or eaten them. The greens were coming along. Lettuce, kale and turnips were up, and like the peas, we had to keep them watered in the fall heat. The onions looked good and should produce a huge crop.

It was inevitable that the recent shooting came up. I passed it off as target practicing gone wrong, but Edna looked skeptical. She knew the truth as she saw everything that went across Bryan's desk, but didn't say anything.

Later at home I fed myself and Kat. We finished the evening in my chair as I wrote, or tried to. I was typing with one hand as Kat demanded the other for her belly rub.

Irene texted me the next morning. She and Sam wanted to come over, and I told her I would be home. I took the tank and picked up some pastries at Mable's and made coffee. They arrived looking like they had not gotten much sleep.

"Any ideas who might be behind your recent truck problem?" I asked.

"I have an idea," Sam said. "If he did not do it, maybe he knows who did."

"Who is he?"

"A former associate of ours. We found the Cove because we were working with him, a guy called Dunder."

"Dunder? What kind of thing is that?"

"It is a who, a man the name of Jack Teal. But everybody calls him Dunder. A farming genius that can grow anything. He was born and raised in the Cove and has a lot of land he both inherited and bought."

"Talking to him should be easy since he's a neighbor."

"We don't talk anymore. We had a personal falling-out."

"Oh. How did he get a name like Dunder?"

"It goes back to when we first started hanging out together," Sam said. "One year he grew a big patch of sugarcane near the river. He decided he was going to start making rum.

This was before we knew we could make a lot of money doing other things. Anyway, he harvested the cane, and we helped him press the juice out. He had gotten an old stainless steel tank from a defunct dairy and hid it in a barn. He dumped the juice and yeast in the tank and we waited for the magic to happen."

"Only it was not so magical," Irene said. "After a few days, we tried to go check on it. The stench was such we could not get within fifty feet of the barn. Later on we figured out he probably used the wrong yeast, plus there were probably wild types in there since we did not sanitize the tank."

"What happened?"

"The tank finally blew the lid off and through the wall. The stink became legendary in the Cove. It was like a dead animal, sewage, and rotten eggs combined. We found out the smelly gunk left over from fermentation of rum was called dunder. That's where the nickname came from. Everyone's called him that since."

"You think he might have killed Lester? You must have a reason."

"As I said, Dunder was one of our associates. He was smart enough to not trust Lester with all his money. But Lester's S&L did hold the mortgages on a lot of land and homes around here. Many were bought out and transferred to other institutions, but apparently some loans were never officially recorded. Lester was taking the payments for himself. One of those shadow loans was to Dunder's parents."

"I could see that being a motivation."

"Dunder used his own money to take care of the situation. Not everybody in Hamilton County was so lucky."

"Then Lester did have a list of enemies," I said. "I'm surprised he lived as long as he did."

"Lester was good at the political side of things, keeping some of the right people happy," Irene said. "It was the only way he stayed out of jail at the time. Even afterward, people thought he had some protection."

"He did have protection," Sam said. "A portion of his illegal profits went into certain politician's pockets. At least until recently."

"I guess the protection expired."

"Definitely."

"Was Lester married?"

"Many times. But lately he was single. Rumors were his money was about gone, along with most of his charm."

"Then he had ex wives. More to add to his enemy list."

"More than you think. He had lots of girlfriends over the years, and all were married."

"OK, so who in the county didn't want to kill him?" Neither Sam nor Irene responded. "Well, at least I've found someone more unpopular than me."

"That is not much consolation, considering the other guy was found murdered on a dish."

"Thanks, Irene."

"Happy to keep you grounded."

"Can you guys get me a list of ex wives, plus the girl-friends and their husbands? Along with any other known enemies likely to kill him?"

"Sure will. We can have it tomorrow."

"Before I forget, I saw a guy pushing a grocery cart when I was leaving your house."

"Yeah that is Duffy. He's not quite right. A childhood accident, or maybe he is neurodivergent. He's been in the Cove forever."

Sam's phone rang. "Sorry, I have to answer this. I'll go outside."

"Is it something serious?" I asked Irene.

"It's not about the truck but about the business," she said. "Somebody needs a delivery because the shipping carrier is late."

"Irene, should I go with Sam to meet with Dunder in case he needs backup?"

"No, not a good idea. If Sam brought someone with him, Dunder would not talk. Besides, Sam can take care of himself."

"I figured he could, but even he might need extra help."

"Sam was in the business years ago because of his brain. But he also got involved in the martial side of it when needed. He had a knack for threatening people in unusual ways. Enough so that he usually did not have to get violent. He is very resourceful."

"Interesting. Why did you guys sever ties with Dunder?"

"This was a long time ago. He liked me even though Sam and I were already a couple. But since we were not married, I guess Dunder thought he could try. Sam was not amused. But I refused to be the reason they were about to get into a fight. Dunder is not a bad guy, and he and Sam were evenly matched. It could have ended badly for both of them. I made Sam leave with me after telling Dunder he had no chance with me. That ended our partnership of the time and we have not talked since."

"Well, let me know if you and Sam need help with Dunder."

"We will. Thanks for the pastries, but this pie is the best. From Mable's? I don't think I've seen it on the menu."

"It is from Vicky Vickers. She stopped by and gave it to me." Seeing the concerned look on Irene's face I went ahead to explain. "No, I don't know why she did it. I'm aware of the old Southern practice of a woman bringing a dish to a man she is interested in. This was not the case, but I have yet to find out what her motives were. And no, I'm not interested in a relationship with her, before you ask."

"Glad you have realized all that. Looks like Sam is off the phone. We need to go and move some product. We will get you that list soon."

"Thanks."

CHAPTER SEVEN

I had a last checkup at the hospital. Normally I would not have bothered going as I knew my neck had healed up without any issues. But I wanted to see Dr. Hoffman again. At her hospital office she checked my neck over.

"I believe you will survive the wound."

"That is good news. You don't see another head sprouting out of there do you?"

"Not today. Even if there was, not my problem. You could probably get the barber shop to treat it."

"I don't think Walter takes insurance. Dr. Hoffman, I'd like to ask you to lunch at Mable's."

"No thanks."

"That was an abrupt declination."

"Dr. Wilder, James, I don't think it is a good idea."

"I'm not asking you on a date. It is lunch with a colleague. Well, sort of colleague. But not a date."

"Still, I don't want to be seen out with someone if it could be confused as a date. There are what, less than 500 people in town? Not that many people in the county. I already have slim chances of connecting with anyone. Going out to lunch with you gives the town gossips ammunition to make us a couple, even if we were not."

"I understand. I have gotten to know how this town works. I do think however, you need to get out and be seen, especially if you want attention from future eligible suitors."

"But I don't have any friends yet."

"I can fix that, at least once or twice. Think about coming to Mable's, where I'll be sitting with two other people. You come in by yourself, sit with us, then I leave first. Nobody will get the wrong idea in that scenario. And you get to start meeting my friends."

"That could work. But it is an elaborate ruse just to get me to lunch."

"True, but it is more about setting you up for the future. An investment in our new doctor."

"Oh, you plan to get me married off and have me stay in town?"

"Maybe. But that is later. Right now it's getting you acclimated and out there in public. Once the older crowd knows you are here, they'll be trying to do all the matchmaking."

"Is that what you will do?"

"Not a chance. I'm fairly new here, so I don't know that many people. Nor do I have any interest in matchmaking. I'm barely solvent on my own."

"The matchmakers did not work their charm and find you a partner?"

"I kind of ran into one on my own. But she is looking to get married, and it is too soon for me to think about that again."

"That's too bad."

"It is OK. Besides, the older crowd has other plans for me."

"Like what?"

"I'm one of their favorites in the betting pool. Or their favorite horse in the race."

"OK, you are going to have to explain that."

"Every time something happens around here, like a murder, I seem to get involved somehow. They bet on me, in regard to whether I solve it, and also when I do."

"That is crazy. No wonder they don't want to burden you with a relationship. Are they betting on you in regard to your own shooting?"

"I'm sure they are."

"This place might be more interesting than just the old history."

"It is. The group I'm talking about is composed of older retired county and town officials, former business leaders, and academics. They have also assisted in the time I've had investigations going. A great resource, if a bit eccentric."

"I can't talk about the current case, but they are probably involved in my recent assistance of the coroner."

"I'm sure they are."

"Wait, are you involved in that?"

"I can't talk about it. But not in the way you might think. The murder itself is not really my concern, but another part of the deceased's life has come up elsewhere and I'm taking a look at that. I'm officially staying out of the investigation."

"Officially? That sounds like a weasel word."

"Weasel word?"

"A word with more than one meaning. For example, you are officially staying out of the main investigation in relation to the authorities, but are involved in other aspects of the case. Possibly even solving it under some circumstances. Am I right?"

"Very well said."

"It must be your hobby in this small, sleepy town."

"Not at all. I don't get involved unless it directly affects me or someone asks me to look at something. I don't go looking for murders or bodies. But lately they seem to wash up on my shore."

"You probably don't go looking. But I bet you are an attractor."

"You mean someone that attracts strangeness? I've been accused of that before."

"Not an accusation, merely an observation. But I believe an accurate one."

"I'd have to agree."

"Are you going to ask me about the case?"

"No, I won't. Those details may have little or no relation to the victim's business deals or property. If it somehow does become important, then somebody else will probably share it."

"I appreciate you not asking me."

"I would not unless there was imminent danger to someone else. But then law enforcement would also be involved, so I still would not have to ask."

She was quiet for a moment. "OK, I agree."

"To what?"

"Lunch at Mable's Diner, under the conditions you already suggested."

"Great. I'll text you once it is set up. Probably do it later this week. Oh, you'll need to give me your number." She raised her eyebrows. "I'll only use it for good, I promise."

"OK. Then you need to get out of here. Or I'll have to charge you for two visits."

"I would not want to overtax my insurance company by cutting into their record profits. Talk to you soon."

An interesting conversation. Did I want to ask her out on a date? I did not think so, but she was intelligent and attractive. A professional looking to set down roots in town. Yet for some reason I was not sure it was a good move for me. Maybe I would reconsider in a year or two. If the townspeople or lack of amenities had not run her off by then. Of course, she might not be interested at all. That was the most likely scenario, so I'd just leave it alone.

At home, Kat was outside, perusing the front for chaseable critters. The specialty of the month was the large, slow grasshoppers. I appreciated when she stalked them, then they flew up at the last second, and she jumped up a foot off the ground to chest-butt them. Fun for us, not as much for the grasshopper. But more than half of them escaped unharmed.

As I stood by my car, I realized I was in the same spot as when the shots were taken at me. The car was in the same spot, or within inches of where it had been parked. The old Land cruiser is a tall vehicle, and I noticed the rack that was now shattered was above my head. I looked over at the distant shooter location, still marked by a piece of tape on a tree branch fluttering in the warm breeze. I remembered being about two feet from the vehicle and starting to reach down for Kat when the first shot was fired.

I pulled out my phone and texted Bryan since I didn't know if he was around today. Two minutes later he rounded the overgrown border between our houses.

"Hey James. What can I do for you?"

"Couldn't you get here quicker? I could have been dead by now."

"I doubt it. You seem to have a knack for ducking at the right time. Besides, I had a fly in my office needing swatted."

"At least you have your priorities sorted. I'm looking at the where the shots came from in relation to where I was at the time. Do you a good idea of the ballistics and bullet paths?"

"I think so. If nothing else I know where the bullets ended up."

"OK, this is about where I was standing, and my car is also in the same place. I was already starting to reach down for Kat when the first shot came."

"Let me walk over in front of you and take a look to match up the bullet paths."

"Can you tell about how close the first bullet was from me?"

"I have a good idea. A few inches high and probably three feet to the left."

"By the time the second bullet came, I was over there and on the ground."

"OK, let me find the spot in the tree where it ended up. I

see it now." He pointed toward the spot with his hand and arm.

"About three feet higher than my head, had I even still been standing there. Nearly ten feet away horizontally. What does that tell you?"

"You had the cheapest and worst assassin, as far as shooting ability, that I've ever seen."

"Or?"

"Or they were not shooting to hit you. If that first shot had not hit the roof rack you might not have even known they were shooting at you."

"Yet somebody did shoot, but quite poorly. Seems more like a warning shot."

"What were they warning you about?"

"No idea. Maybe they just don't like me."

"A viable hypothesis."

"Did you get the list I emailed over?"

"I did. Edna has assigned it to the deputies. Each one gets a few people and will check on their availability on the day of the shooting. We've already crossed two off as we know they were out of town with their families on vacation."

"Millard also has it and his gang are checking. They had their own list as well, so it should be comprehensive."

"I don't suppose they would share it with me?"

"They might if you ask, but I doubt it. Don't feel bad, they probably won't give it to me either."

"We will just have to do it without them."

"You hear any more about that body in the dish? I believe you told me his name was Lester."

"Not much. The interim sheriff has kept it very quiet. His deputies have been unusually quiet, so he must have threatened them about leaks. I do know the state has the body for further testing. Must be something unusual for that to happen."

"How is John Dixon doing in the job? I know he was the new Warm Springs chief only a short time before getting the sheriff job."

"I think he is fine. Made sense to get appointed to it since he didn't even have a staff yet in Warm Springs. He'd already passed all the checks to get the Warm Springs job. Plenty of experience yet from out of the area, so he was not tainted by the old Jefferson Jackson regime."

"Hope it works out. You thought any more about running for sheriff?"

"A little. It appeals to me professionally, but I have serious doubts. I like my dinners at home and ball games with the kids too much. What really scares me is all the political stuff, running a campaign and raising money, all while trying to do the actual job."

"It is a bit much, especially for a man with a young family. Maybe John will do it for a while, then you take over once he retires in a few years."

"We will see. It is a matter of hitting the sweet spot—not too young and not too old for that kind of job."

"Yep, that applies to a lot of things."

CHAPTER EIGHT

I was having a simple breakfast at home. Strong, sweet coffee along with a bowl of fruit sprinkled with granola and covered with kefir. I finished the coffee and thought about another while toying with the half-eaten bowl. A lot was going on right now and I had a dozen different things to do. The problem was I had no good way of prioritizing them. But I needed to, or I'd drive myself crazy. Early retirement was becoming more full and stressful than my former job.

The one item I could move down the list was investigating my shooting. I still needed to know what was happening, but I did not feel there was an imminent threat. Fine, eleven more things to sort. I dumped the bowl, rinsed my cup and went out to start the day. Maybe things would keep happening and throwing themselves in my way, so I wouldn't have to choose what to tackle, much less order it.

But until then, I would do none of the things on the list and go walk instead. It was still too warm to brave the jungle to the Pine Mountain Trail, but was cool enough for a long walk around campus even in midday. This morning was even cooler, so I set off. Unfortunately, my mind was still locked on the things yet to be done. I let that part of my brain churn, while another part enjoyed the sights, sounds, and smells of nature.

Not many plants and trees were blooming, but the scent of muscadines was in the air. Purple carcasses of fallen grapes were on the road and lending the smell, at least until the deer or squirrels snarfed them up. The warm asphalt helped lift the aroma. I wondered if some of them were already fermenting alcohol while sitting on the heated pavement. That could explain the crazy squirrel behavior.

Clumps of thyme along the side of the road were covered with small flowers. Not exactly blue, but with shades of purple and pink in the blossom. The flowers were not large enough to scent the air, but I stopped to pull off some leaves. Whatever variety it was, it was less aromatic than newer selected varieties, which I appreciated. The leaves were also larger than what I typically saw with modern varieties. I assume it was an older, less developed variety that escaped from the cottage gardens over the past century.

Then the annoying part of my brain broke in with the list of things needed to be done. I came up with a rough plan and schedule just to stop the howling in my head. Although the sound was more of an insistent, high-pitched whine. I would do a few things in order and other things would work in as I felt like doing them. Already knowing that events would likely skew or invalidate my plans within hours or days.

My walk ended as I spied Kat in the front yard and went to greet her. She accepted a few head scratches and a back scrub. Then she was off to the side yard to find more grasshoppers. That was my cue to get back to my life and begin checking items off the must do list.

The easy one was obvious. I grabbed an empty and clean pie dish and drove just out of town. I found the gravel driveway that led to the Vickers' house. Formerly Doyle's, but now Vicky's. Passing through a grove of trees masking the house from the road, I saw a brick two-story, similar to other houses along the road. A large garage just off to the side. There were bare spots of dirt about the size and shape of cars in the sparse lawn. I remember someone telling me Doyle used to keep junk cars to make the neighbors, most of them family, mad. I was expecting a pack of barking dogs but they never materialized. I saw the car she had driven to my house, so I assumed she was home.

I parked beside it and waited another ten seconds to see if hounds or attack dogs appeared. They did not, so I went to the front door, pie dish in hand. I knocked and waited a few seconds before the door opened.

"Hi Vicky. I brought your dish back."

"Thank you James, but that was not necessary."

"It was, actually. First of all, you needed the dish back. But I've also been worried about you."

"What? I'm not sure what you mean."

"You were gracious enough to bring me a wonderful pie, but you seemed distracted, or maybe anxious about something."

"I'm OK."

"How are you doing? Really."

"I… I'm not so great."

"Do you want to talk about it?"

"No, not right now. It's just…" She began to tear up. "I can't talk right now."

"OK. Would you like to come over to my house for dinner? We can talk and I promise what ever you say will be kept confidential. Or if you need help with something I'll try to assist."

"Thank you James, I just might do that."

"Can I text you to set it up?

"Yes, OK. Here is my number."

"Good, then when you come over, we can talk, eat, or both."

"I'll be looking forward to it."

"Are you sure? I do put on a nice dinner."

"That would be nice. Thank you."

As I left, I was not sure whether I had just made a date or begun a confessional process. Perhaps both. But I hoped she would not see it that way. My preference would have been to meet her at Mable's Diner for lunch. Yet I knew she would have been hesitant to talk in public. At my house, over food, I thought she would be more forthcoming.

Nor did I want the town thinking I was seeing Vicky. We both had enough problems without the town gossip chain weighing in. I was conscious of Donna's advice. Now I had to decide whether or not to tell Donna before Vicky came over. I did not owe Donna the courtesy since we were not dating, but I felt I did owe it to her as a concerned friend. If I waited until afterward to tell her I doubted it would go well.

Might as well rip off the bandaid and get it over with. I dialed Donna and she quickly answered.

"Hey Donna, how are you doing?"

"I'm good and hope you are as well. What are you up to?"

"I just dropped off the clean pie dish at the good widow Vicker's house."

"Oh? Did she lure you into her web?

"No, but when I asked her if anything was wrong she basically began crying."

"That does not sound like Vicky. Was she playing you? Or trying to win your affection?"

"I don't know. I'm not always the most aware person for recognizing when someone is interested in me. But I get no vibes whatsoever from her that she sees me as a romantic interest."

"You are a bit dense in that area. But I think if she was after you there would not be much question about her intentions."

"I agree. Something is going on with her, and somehow it involves me. She also might know something I would like to know."

"The identity of who was in Doyle's truck the night they dumped Mike Vicker's body?"

"Yes. I still think she knows, and maybe I can help her with whatever is bothering her. She might be more inclined to tell me."

"How are you planning to bring that up?"

"Well, I have invited her to dinner at my house."

"James, I understand what you are doing and why. But part of me wants to scream at you right now."

"I know and that is why I'm telling you upfront what I am planning."

"You know, this is not my business. I have no right to tell you what to do."

"Actually, you do, and I appreciate it."

"I don't get it. We are not dating anymore."

"But we are friends. I want your input and even to yell at me if you think I deserve it. More importantly, I want you to sit outside my house with a fire extinguisher when Vicky comes over. If you see her make a move, then you burst in and hose her down."

Donna laughed. "That would be fun, I guess. Thanks for letting me know about the plans with Vicky. I trust you to handle it without me or the fire extinguisher."

"You are welcome. I wanted you to know before it happened, and certainly before you heard it from the town's gossip vine."

"Come on, you aren't that important. At least not until you father a child with her."

"Hey, there will be no talk of fathering a child with anyone. Although someday I might foster a stray cat."

"Yes, stick with the cats, James."

"I will, because I think they are a lot safer. Oh, I have a favor to ask you."

"Go ahead, as long as it does not involve Vicky."

"No, this is about Dr. Hoffman, our newest doctor at the hospital."

"Oh, I met her at a luncheon last week. She seems nice."

"I am glad you agree. Could you vouch for me and tell her I'm good boyfriend material?" There was silence on the phone. My joke might not be as funny as I thought. "I'm kidding, Donna. Sorry about the bad joke."

"You better be."

"I'm trying to get her to meet people in the town outside of work. Part of an effort to immerse her in the community, and maybe get her to stay here long term. I was thinking of meeting Millard at Mable's for lunch. I'd like you to come in and sit with us, then she comes in and joins us."

"Ah, I get it. A social occasion but nobody thinks romance is going on."

"Exactly. I'll leave early by myself to keep the gossip down."

"You don't have to do that."

"Probably better if I do. Keeps you and the doctor out of the gossip chain. And I'm sure Millard won't mind."

"Sure, I'll do it. Text me when, but give me a day's notice."

"Thanks, I will."

CHAPTER NINE

Next on my list was going to see Sam and Irene. We had lunch at their house and they gave me a list of names containing people likely to want to harm Lester. It was a long list.

"I don't know most of these people," I said.

"We thought you might not," Irene said. "We added a little background for each name, just a few sentences. Who they are and why they might be suspects."

Sam slid a usb flash drive over to me. "I thought you would prefer a digital version."

"I appreciate that. On the way over I realized I need to know a lot more about Lester. That would make it a little easier to evaluate suspects."

"We also put that on the flash drive," Irene said. "But we

can discuss it as well. That might save you from having later questions."

"Was Lester from the area?"

"Yes, born and raised in Woodbury. He came from a family that has been in the area since the early settlement days. They had their ups and downs, but became powerful again with the pimento age of Woodbury. They had lots of acreage in peppers and owned one of the processing plants. That money and influence greased Lester's way into the Savings and Loan."

"We've already told you about the illegal activities he conducted there," Sam added.

"What kind of person was he?" I asked.

"We always heard he was spoiled as a kid. By the time we met him he was a confidence man. Charming and could talk anyone into anything. But only for a while, because within weeks or months you would realize his lies were not consistent. I don't recall him ever suffering any repercussions for his actions."

"What has he been doing since the Savings and Loan failure?"

"Various small businesses, including financial management."

"Seems like people here would know about his past and not give him money."

"He only catered to newcomers. Last I heard that business had been closed."

"Did he swindle anyone in a big way?"

"Probably. The ones we think he swindled more recently are on the list and summary, but I doubt we have everyone."

"If there was one person in Woodbury that knew him well and likely got conned, who would it be?"

"You could choose from several people. I know three business owners that are newer and had dealings with Lester. A concrete manufacturer that came into town about ten years ago, the sporting goods place on the edge of town, and the advertising guy."

"Who is the advertising guy and where is his business?"

"His name is Charles Robinson. His office is downtown and his yard is on the highway toward the Cove."

"Why does an advertising person need a yard?"

"He does big stuff. Mostly billboards in the region. He also does signs for businesses." That was interesting, as he had access to tall ladders or lifts.

"You mentioned before Lester had ex wives. Anyone willing to kill him and able to put him in the dish?"

"I don't think so. But they could have hired someone. The husband's of his several girlfriends are a better set of suspects."

"I believe I have a lot of work to do. Yet I doubt many of the potential suspects have the means to hoist Lester thirty feet in the air, plus themselves, in order to write something in blood."

"That is true," Sam said. "Have you heard yet what the word was?"

"Not yet. But it can't stay quiet much longer. Somebody will eventually tell somebody and it will get out."

"I can't believe they bled Lester out to do something like that," Irene said.

"That is another clue," I said. "Whoever did it really hated him to make it that personal. And they had to be physical enough to make it happen."

"That should shorten the list."

"I remember you guys saying Duffy has been in the Cove forever. How do you know him?"

"We have seen him for years," Irene said. "At least once a week he's walking along the river and the edges of the fields. At first we thought he was homeless, but he's not. We offered him a place in our loft out in our outbuilding but he didn't need it. Even so, we give him food. Fruit and vegetables from our garden mostly, sometimes a pie or cake. Make sure he has a good coat in the winter."

"I've been in the Cove a few times," I said. "I have never seen him until now. But it seems I would have noticed him since he is on the main road with a grocery cart."

"That is something new he has been doing," Sam said. "He's only been on the road pushing the cart the last couple of weeks."

"Where does he go with it, and what does he haul?"

"No idea. I don't remember ever seeing anything in the cart. Maybe he just likes pushing it."

"Seems like he would be picking something up."

"The only thing I know he collects are feathers. Oh, and Native American artifacts. Probably why he walks the river and fields. Good places to find feathers and artifacts. I heard he has one of the best collections of American Indian artifacts in this part of the state. But neither of those items requires a shopping cart."

"But his passion is feathers?"

"Yes, anything and everything that are feathers. Why do you ask?"

"I have a feeling I should talk to Duffy. I imagine few people really notice him. But if he is in the Cove full time and outside, he probably knows a lot more about what happens here than most people."

"Good luck with that, and keep your patience with him."

"Why?"

"I believe he is quite intelligent, but he speaks different from most people. It takes a minute to decipher what he is saying."

"Good to know. Thanks for the list and I'll start working on it."

As I drove out of the Cove, I thought about who I should talk to first. The concrete company would have scaffolding, the sporting goods place had deer stand ladders, and the billboard company would have some kind of equipment to reach heights. All could have gotten Lester's body in the dish. But the scaffolding would be much more effort to put up and take down, so I'd hold off talking to the concrete company for now. I noticed a familiar motorcycle for a short time, then I lost it on the way to Woodbury.

I went past the billboard advertising yard on the way into town. On the way out toward Warm Springs, I went past the sporting goods place. Both businesses were possibilities to get Lester on the dish, and I would start with them first. Just not today.

Instead I went home and took a walk on campus, around the outer loop. I had a mission to complete if Millard was home. I wanted to give him Sam and Irene's list so the Octo-posse could work their magic. I would keep the summary for myself until I checked it to make sure it contained nothing that could be traced back to Sam and Irene.

"Hi Millard," I said loudly as I saw him on his porch.

"Hey James, come on up and help me kill the lemonade."

"Thanks." He handed me a glass as I settled into the rocking chair next to his. "Millard, I have something new for the Octoposse to look into."

"Oh, are you getting into trouble again?"

"No not me. But I did want to help someone else out. They prefer to remain anonymous at this time."

"The plot thickens. What have you got?"

"This is a list of potential suspects. People that might have killed Lester Owens."

"Now that is a hot topic. Our group has been talking about the murder a lot, but we have not done anything official yet. How good is this list?"

"I think it is quite good. People he swindled, mortgagees he cheated, some illegal associations not widely known, ex wives, and the husbands of women he had dalliances with."

He gave me a speculative look as he ran down the list of names. "James, this is a goldmine. We can work with this. But for someone to have this information they must have been in cahoots somehow with Lester and known him for a long time. We all knew him but I don't think we could have put this comprehensive list together."

"Like I said, I'm doing someone a favor. They would like Lester's killer caught."

"A concerned citizen. Either a good samaritan or someone likely to be a top suspect, I'd say."

"Thus the wish to remain anonymous."

"You keep interesting company for a quiet retiree."

"My life hasn't been quiet for a while."

"I know. Having you around has been entertaining."

"Possibly not the word I would have used. But speaking of that, I have a favor to ask."

"This should be interesting."

"Dr Hoffman over at the hospital is new in town and needs to meet people. I offered, but she declined as she didn't want town gossips putting us together. But I convinced her that meeting several people at Mable's, seemingly by chance, would be an innocent gathering. I'd like you and Donna to help me out with lunch."

"You mean I have to have lunch with you and two attractive young women? Count me in."

"I thought you would somehow find it within you to accept."

I met Millard in Mable's for lunch the following day. We had a table for four since we were expecting company and we were already drinking iced tea. A few minutes later Donna walked in and we invited her to sit. It was a table with chairs on all four sides, like a card table, so it was not awkward for any of us. Donna ordered tea when Dr. Hoffman walked in. We invited her over, and she sat with us as planned.

We all ordered and Millard held court while we listened. Dr. Hoffman had ordered us to call her Lisa, and she was peppering Millard with questions on the history of the town and campus. He was more than happy to answer everything, throwing in an occasional embellishment. I was happy because I didn't have to talk. Customers at other tables were listening as well, and Millard introduced Lisa to all within earshot.

Lottie brought her typical commentary to our table to get our orders. It would not be Mable's without her.

"What are you two lovely ladies doing with these two old coots?" Lottie asked.

"Old coot?" asked Millard. "I'll have you know I'm more of a mallard. Coots are so out of date as water birds go."

"OK, so you aren't a bird. My emphasis was more on the 'old' portion of old coot, anyway. James, I know you have more sense than to hang out with Millard."

"You wound me, Lottie," Millard said.

"Well, aren't you the oldest one at the table? Would you like it better if I called you the wise one?"

"I believe I would."

"Then you wait til last while I get the orders from everyone else first. That will give you time to think of something wise to say. I know you need a moment."

"Millard, is that what dating in your 80s looks like?" I asked.

"It is what successful dating looks like. Banter and intelligent insults are what keeps the home fires burning."

Lottie made an insulting sound and took our orders. Lisa quickly went back to asking history questions. It was obvious history was her passion and possibly her hobby. Millard was in his element.

The food came, and the conversation took a pause. Donna and Lisa began talking about sports. Lisa did not play golf but did play tennis. With Donna's sports skills I was not surprised that she also played tennis. They made a date for a morning match later in the week. Even though fall was here, the day's heat would get uncomfortable after the morning.

"What about pickleball?" I interjected. "Something less strenuous for us elders?"

"I've been wanting to try it," Donna said.

"Can't do it with my hip," Millard said.

We all looked at Lisa for her input. "Is it easier than tennis? If so, I'm game to give it a try."

"The gym on campus has courts set up every Thursday, from noon to closing at nine," I said. "We just need a fourth and we will be ready."

"I really don't know anyone yet that I can ask," Lisa said.

"I have a couple I can ask," Donna said.

"I can ask Sam and Irene, as she already comes to campus to walk," I said. "Maybe a couple of others."

"I can bring the cheering section," Millard said. "Lottie might even want to play."

"I'll text everyone and see what afternoon or evening works the next couple of weeks. We'll have a court reserved and will be playing in air conditioning. Much more civilized than the game of tennis."

As food dwindled, I made myself scarce and left first. I thought it went well, but I still had lots of things to do.

CHAPTER TEN

Somewhere along the way to Watkinsville I realized I was on a feather quest. I was going to get some special feathers for my project. I really needed to talk to Duffy, and based on what Sam and Irene had told me, feathers might be the currency to make that happen. Otherwise I did not think Duffy would talk to a stranger.

Of course, humans had been going on feather quests for thousands of years. Feathers were valued throughout history for various reasons, predominately ornamental and sometimes martial in the case of arrow fletching. They were also a prized trade item and were carried along the Silk Road. In the New World, turkeys were domesticated in Central America and Mexico not for their meat, but for their plumage. Feathers were a renewable resource, because the birds regrew them once plucked.

Feathers fascinated humans with their colors and patterns. Barred, stippled, and mottled versions of flight feathers, contour feathers, and semi-plumes. I once owned a two-volume set someone had written and illustrated about avian integument, and a lot of it was about feathers. Way too much information, honestly.

There was still a big market for feathers. They were used in the entertainment and fashion industry and in the sporting goods market. And, of course, plain old goose and duck down to stuff pillows and comforters.

The colleague I was visiting grew a variety of birds only for their feathers. About eighty percent of his business was the sport fishing industry, mainly wealthy trout fisherman and companies making flies. He also sold some to collectors and a niche market in the fashion industry that produced a few, very expensive feather wigs and ornaments for select clients around the world.

South of Watkinsville, I drove on rural roads that were becoming a lot less rural. The area had been discovered and that meant development. Larger tracts of land were sold off for horse farms or subdivisions with expensive homes. At one time the country roads were so light on traffic I could ride twenty miles on a bicycle and not see more than ten cars. Now there were ten cars lined up at stop signs, and during peak hours there might be fifty cars.

I was glad to pull into the long gravel road leading to my destination. There was no sign or mailbox, as the owner preferred privacy. I only knew about the place from my time at the university. An enterprising student who inherited the land I was on realized, like the Aztecs and Mayas, there was an opportunity in growing birds for feathers.

The drive ended in front of a wide one-story building painted green. It blended well into the surrounding forest. I knew there were several long thin buildings running straight back from behind the building before me. There was one door and two windows, otherwise just lots of green concrete block. I knocked on the door and went in.

The room was painted bright white, and the walls were lined with probably a hundred picture frames. Within the frames were feathers, lots of feathers. Every shape, size, color, and pattern was shown in the frames. A small plate on each listed the type of bird and type of feather. Some picture frames were paired, as juvenile birds might have different feathers than adults, and males might have different feathers than females. It was an impressive display designed to get the attention of the few customers invited to the feather factory.

A receptionist came out and told me the owner would be with me in a moment. A man I once knew as a student, Richard, came out and we spent a few minutes discussing mutual acquaintances. Then I told him I needed about thirty feathers. Nothing too exotic, but somewhat showy. Best from types of birds common to North America, or even hybrids from the region. He nodded, left, and came back in five minutes with a black case. He opened it and showed me the selection. I thanked him and asked the price. He declined payment after he asked my intentions and learned I was giving them away. He would only charge me if I were using them to make a profit. I thanked him again and left.

Since I was close to Athens, I drove to campus. I wanted to see my old colleague Al, the one who helped decipher the manuscript I had found under the guest cottage. He might be able to steer me to the right person at the university doing field archaeology research. South Campus looked the same as always. Little new building was happening as most of the available space was now filled, and new construction was directed further out on South Milledge Avenue. Besides, the football team might need another two or three practice fields on campus.

I found Al in the squat building and office he had inhabited for years. He was expecting me due to an earlier text I'd sent. His office was crowded with stacks of papers as always. Reminded me of my old campus office. We traded pleasantries, and I got to business. It was still a long ride back to Warm Springs.

"Al, have you ever worked with any of the anthropologists or archaeologists on North Campus?

"We have. One anthropologist recently brought us some manuscripts to scan. After the letter you brought in, I realized we could expand our services, and let the department head know what we could offer. We also looked at some fabric fragments from a colonial settlement in North Carolina. We can nondestructively evaluate what dyes the colonists were using. We also looked at some Native American basket fragments for both identification of the willow or rush used, plus a dark dye that was used. Why do you ask?"

"I need to find out if anyone is using a portable ground penetrating radar system in Georgia. I'm looking for something buried on the Roosevelt Warm Springs campus and need to narrow down the area where we might need to dig."

"Looking for one of the bodies mentioned in the letter?"

"Not exactly. But there was mention of a leather suitcase with belongings that was buried after the incident. If I can find that then I won't have to go searching for actual bodies to prove the letter is factual." I was telling Al a lie, but I did not want to involve him in digging up a murdered body. I had no idea if it would still be a legal issue, but I suspected it could.

"That makes sense. I can call a couple of people and let you know."

"Thanks Al. I'm heading back to Warm Springs, so call me anytime."

"I will. Keep a shovel handy."

I stopped at my usual favorite coffee shop in Watkinsville. Banana nut bread and two coffees, my usual. Al called me before I left the store. That was quick service.

"James, I talked to one of the researchers running an archaeological dig in Georgia. Turns out he is on the Flint River, south of where you are in Warm Springs. Very hush-hush, as their regular dig unearthed some much older artifacts."

"Let me guess, the carbon dating came back somewhere between 18,000 and 30,000 years ago."

"Exactly, how did you know?"

"It is happening a lot these days. The old generation of archaeologists keeps trying to suppress evidence to protect their theory that humans were only in America since 11,000 years ago. But too much evidence is showing up that the habitation of the Americas is much older."

"He mentioned something about that. Keeping his dig secret for a while longer is important to him until they have multiple confirmations of their dates. Otherwise the old professors will skewer him."

"I've heard that before. Most of the older professors stick

with the Clovis-first theory, despite it now being widely disproven. Dangerous for a younger professor to prove them wrong."

"Anyway, he has two ground penetrating radar or GPR units down there that they are not using at the moment. Since using them to define the site, they are now concentrating on digging and cataloging finds. I'll text you his information. He seemed interested when I told him you were at the Roosevelt campus. One of his students really wants to research the ancient history of the springs."

"That makes sense. I imagine Native Americans were aware of and using the warm springs for many centuries. It would not surprise me if there was an ancient site in Warm Springs."

"I believe he thinks the same. Give him a call and I imagine he will be happy to lend you a GPR and a graduate student."

"Thanks Al."

I called the number that Al had texted. The young professor answered, and I told him about my project. I had an area about ten by twenty feet and thought there was a suitcase buried four or five feet down. Or at least what was left of one after eighty years. I told him there was an adjacent water main in case that would interfere with the machine.

He thought for a moment and said the water main would not be an issue. It could be a positive and offer a clear boundary and marker for the computer algorithms. A decayed suitcase might be difficult but the disturbed ground around it should be noticeable. He could send two graduate students and a machine up in a few days when they took a break from the current dig. I thanked him then he asked if I knew anyone on the Warm Springs campus he could contact for a future dig. My buddy Ison could help him, and if not, Ison could find the right person to contact. Due to multiple jurisdictions on and adjacent to the campus it would be fun to chase different people for authorization, but I would help with that when he was ready to try. He thanked me and hung up.

Well, that was another step closer to possibly finding something under the garden. It might prove or disprove the letter. In a way, I hoped to find nothing. It might invalidate the letter, but then I would not have to dig up what little remained of a corpse and then decide what to do with it.

In the Cove on my way home I saw Duffy pushing the grocery cart along the road. It was empty as before. I was curious what he was doing, but I needed to know him better before asking questions about his business. I had hung up three nice feathers on a clip hanging from my rear-view mirror.

I stopped a few feet away from him and rolled the passenger-side window down. He did not look like he wanted to talk to me.

"Hi, could you tell me where the river is?"

He pointed down the road without saying anything.

"Do you know if that is where the Native Americans put the rocks in the river to make a fish weir?" I thought Duffy must have some knowledge of the river.

"The stones like this?" He put his hands in the shape of a V.

"Yes, that place."

He stepped closer to the car. "Go that way. Make for the

dirt track by the yellow house. Near the river is a large sycamore. Another hundred steps is where you go."

"Thanks." I saw Duffy staring at the feathers. One of them was a large tail feather from a heritage turkey. White with unusual black patterns.

"Those are nice," he said.

"I like to collect feathers. I am glad you like them. Say, do you collect feathers too? I have more feathers at home. I can bring them by if you would like to look at them."

"Oh yes. Yes please. Any feathers are good. I have many but there are so many to see."

"Would you like this one? I have others." It was a nice grouse feather. Black, brown, and white stripes with a black tip. I didn't know if there were any grouse in the Cove, but it was similar enough to other game birds he might have seen or collected feathers from.

"Yes please, thank you. Yes please. But I will trade you. Do you like this one?" He pulled a small, well-carved flint arrowhead about the size of a quarter from his pocket.

"Oh, that is a nice one. That might be worth two feathers."

"This one is fine, just fine, yes. Only one feather. I have lots of stones to trade if you have more feathers."

"When I come back, I will bring more and then you decide if you like them."

"More is good, yes. Would you bring that one back?" He pointed to the large turkey feather.

"Yes I will. I'll drive back over in a day or two. Would you like to meet here at a certain time?"

"You see the sun over the hill there? I walk here when the sun is there."

"OK, about this same time but in a one or two days. If you

see this car, it will be me. And with some feathers. Oh, my name is James."

"I am called Duffy."

"Take care now."

He nodded his head and went back to his cart as I drove away. That went better than expected. I was not sure he would talk to me, but the feather seemed to work. Best of all, I got a nice arrowhead. There were lots of them around but I always enjoyed every one I had ever found or been given.

CHAPTER ELEVEN

Before Vicky arrived, I wondered how the evening would go. My hope was that we would have some food and talk about what was bothering her. Depending on how that went I might ask her about Doyle's companion in the truck. Then she would leave and I would decide what to do with whatever information I got. But people were not predictable so that made me slightly nervous.

For dinner with Vicky I decided to go neutral. Not a heavy meal with steak, nor one involved with fancy poultry. Just something easy and light. Pasta it was.

But not any lazy pasta of boiled noodles and thick meat and tomato sauce. Just a few ingredients was all that were needed for a spectacular dish. But since there were only a few ingredients, they all had to be excellent, or the dish was doomed to mediocrity. My recipe included sun-dried tomatoes, pine nuts, olive oil, balsamic vinegar, and noodles. That was all that was necessary for an excellent dish with a little preparation. I'd eaten the dish in Verona, Italy, and remembered how great it was. Fresh, simple, and wonderful.

It was important to use good quality sun-dried tomatoes. Too many on the market were dried leather and would not soften regardless of how long they were soaked. I didn't want to spend a half hour of extra time at dinner chewing tough tomatoes. Trial and error was required to find a good and consistent brand. I now only used those bottled in olive oil. But those could not be gooey, which was almost as a bad as too chewy. I tried to buy what I knew worked, even though they were more expensive.

Pine nuts were another important ingredient. Most pine nuts were imported from countries with lower quality standards than I would accept. Thus many batches of relatively cheap pine nuts were musty and past their prime. Only good quality nuts, fresh and slightly crispy, were right for a simple pasta dish. Of course those came at a hefty price.

Olive oil was important, as old oil tasted slightly rancid. It was hard for me to decide on a great one, but there were lots of good ones. Price did not always guarantee quality, so tasting a few different oils was necessary. It was essential to try lots of categories or types of oil. There was plenty of variation among the many bottlers, distributors, and brands. But most were acceptable.

Balsamic vinegar was similar to olive oil, where choosing one among the large variety available was difficult. I looked for one not too thick, and not too sweet. Beyond that it was too much trouble to sift through all the options. I did not even use it all the time, only when the tomatoes were under par.

Ironically, the pasta noodles, the bulk of the dish, were possibly the least important item. Sure, if there was a good local-made fresh pasta available, I'd make use of it. But if not, I'd pop open a box of mass-produced stuff and throw in a couple of tricks. Most people could not tell the difference after I worked a little incredibly simple magic.

My tricks were to cook the pasta in the least amount of water possible, so the pasta would be finished cooking as the last of the water was evaporating. The method improved the taste as most of the unevaporated liquids absorbed into the pasta. It required attention and a lot of extra stirring. Then I'd reduce heat and add a little dairy, something like half-and-half, whole milk, or even whipping cream. I just used less of the good stuff. If I did not have any of those, a small amount of good butter would help. But too much would overpower the pasta. Once the dairy addition was soaked into the noodles, they were done and ready to dump into the skillet of the good stuff.

Preparing the dish itself was simple. Add oil, sauté at a reasonable temperature to protect the oil, and add the pine nuts. I wanted a little color on the pine nuts from the hot oil. But not too much as it was important to neither burn the nuts or scorch the oil. Then add the tomatoes, but not for too long to keep them from overcooking. Hot with a tender texture was perfect. Dump in the noodles, continue heating for a couple of minutes, and it was done.

I quartered a head of iceberg lettuce and made two wedge salads. With some homemade ranch dressing, a piece of bacon crumbled over it, and a sprinkle of fresh parmesan shreds and it was ready to go.

I had iced tea and white wine, because I did not know if Vicky drank alcohol or not. I planned to stick with tea. After I'd invited her I realized she might think this was a date, although I didn't intend for it to be romantic. The less wine the better.

The dessert was as simple as the meal. Thinly sliced pound cake from Mable's, layered with some Maine blueberries plus some strawberries I had frozen as fresh two months previous. Some homemade whipped cream with sugar and vanilla in each layer. And that was all that was needed to complete the meal.

Vicky arrived, dressed nicely but not provocatively. I assumed she would not dress in that manner, but I had a slight doubt probably planted by Donna's distrust of Vicky. I opened the door for her and she stepped in tentatively. Whatever was on her mind was still bothering her.

"Vicky, thanks for coming over."

"I appreciate the invitation. I don't get home-cooked dinners very often, other than cooking it myself. I hope it was not too much trouble."

"Not at all. I like to cook, especially for guests. Cooking for myself gets boring."

"I know what you mean."

"Would you like something to drink? I have tea or wine."

"Tea would be nice." Good, maybe she was thinking the same thing I was. No alcohol and keep things normal. Just two people eating and talking. I poured two glasses of tea and handed one to her.

"Dinner will be ready in about five minutes. Feel free to look around while I finish up."

"Thanks, I will. I always liked these old cottages but I've never been in one."

"This one probably isn't the nicest on campus, and certainly is not the largest, but it works for me."

"It is nice. I can tell it is old, but it doesn't feel used up."

"That is a good way of putting it." I finished sautéing the dish and dumped in the pasta. "It has lasted longer than the previous three owners. I hope you like pasta and salad."

"I'm sure it will be fine. I see you are finishing up. Where is the salad? I'll put it on the table."

"They are in the refrigerator. No rush, though. In Italy you might get served pasta before the salad. Here I put out both at the same time and you can decide how, or rather when, to eat one or the other."

We sat to eat and enjoy the simple meal. After a moment, Vicky gave a low growl. I was not sure what to make of it.

"James, sorry about that. But the pasta is great. I was expecting a thick meat sauce with hamburger or venison. And the salad dressing is great."

"Thanks. I make the dressing. And I found the pasta dish in Italy. Taught me the sauce does not have to be heavy on tomato, meat, or cream to be good."

"You are right about that. After dinners at that Italian chain I didn't realize how good simple could be."

"It is good. Plus you can add something like spinach if you'd like something green. I can spend a few seconds and write down the recipe if you want to try it at home. You can put it together in fifteen minutes."

"I'd like that."

We ate and made more small talk, mostly about the history of the cottage and the campus. As the dessert dwindled, I decided to start the real conversation.

"Vicky, the two times I've seen you lately, I thought you were upset or worried about something. I don't know what it might be, but if you wanted to talk about it, I might be able to help."

"I don't think you can help. But I am worried."

"Please tell me. Maybe talking will help if nothing else."

"You remember when I talked to you before about Doyle? Right before he was killed. You mentioned if Doyle was gone I might get the house and property. Maybe most of it if he went to jail."

"Yes, I remember. If it wasn't involved in his crimes or no tax issues."

"I got to thinking about all he had done, and how mean he was to me. I went to see Sheriff Jackson. I thought I could sweet-talk him. Then he would arrest Doyle."

"Whatever you said it must have got the sheriff's attention."

"I never meant for them to kill him. I thought they would arrest him. Then I could get the house and property."

"From everything I know, the sheriff did not have Doyle killed based on anything you said. It was business gone bad. But whether he was arrested or killed, I assume you did get the house and land."

"I thought I had. But not now. Last month about when I thought everything was settled a woman lawyer from Atlanta came to my house. Told me she was going to take Doyle's business, the house and the land. Any vehicles or other property he had. Everything. She was going to confiscate it for the state and sell it off."

"I'm not a lawyer, but I don't think that sounds right. If the house and land were not used in any way to commit a crime, nor were they paid for by criminal activity, they should be safe. But laws might have changed."

"They must have. She told me everything was going to be frozen, including bank accounts. Even mine, which Doyle had nothing to do with."

"Do you have a lawyer?"

"Right now I can't afford one."

"Vicky, I need to check into some things. I also know someone that might could help you on the legal side."

"I would appreciate anything you could do."

"What is the woman lawyer's name from Atlanta?"

"Pamela Foster."

"Thanks. I should know something soon. Could you give me a dollar?"

"Uh, what?"

"I need to take it to someone. Consider it a legal retainer. It is a long story but I think this person could really help you."

"OK, here is a dollar."

"Thanks. I'd use my own, but it has to come from you."

"James... I'm sorry."

"For what?"

"For... never mind. Thanks again for trying to help."

"You are welcome."

"Thanks for the great food. I need to go now."

"Thanks again for having dinner. I'll let you know as soon as I can set something up for your legal advice."

"I'll talk to you soon."

She nearly bolted from the house and to her car. Another strange encounter with Vicky. Something still was not right.

I needed to go see Larry in Hamilton. The name of the lawyer from Atlanta seemed familiar from somewhere, and if they were sleazy, I was sure Larry would know them. Despite his disbarment, I also knew he was an excellent lawyer, or had been.

A few minutes later another car appeared in the driveway. From the window I knew it who it was.

"Hi Donna. Would you like to come in?"

"Hello James. No thanks, this won't take but a minute."

"Sure, let's talk."

"I came by earlier and saw Vicky's car. I know you are not interested in Vicky, nor she you. I know it in my head, but the truth is I still have a hard time dealing with anything that has to do with her. I need to be away from all this until it is over, whatever her interest is in talking to you."

"You are telling me that you won't be around for a while. When Vicky disappears from my normal life, though, things will be better."

"I really don't want to be like this. I know it is irrational. But I see her or hear her name, and I go right back to my divorce and some of the reasons for it."

"It is painful and you don't need to be reminded of it."

"Exactly. I have an emotional flare and it takes me a little while to get over it."

"I understand. I think Vicky should be out of my orbit quite soon. When that happens, I'll call you. Then we can take a walk and see how you feel."

"I think that would be best. Again, I'm not upset about anything you've done. This is my issue."

"I know, and it is fine. Your feelings are valid and I respect that you need a little distance right now. We will talk soon."

"Thank you for understanding, James."

"Bye Donna."

I had better get on with the unpleasantness I was due to have with Vicky. It had to be done, now that I was almost sure what the problem was. Perhaps after that things would get better with Donna. I did not want to lose her as a friend.

CHAPTER TWELVE

"Hi Larry."

"Hey James. Are you here to distract me from my ball therapy?" Larry was throwing a tennis ball, bouncing it off the floor, then the wall, and back to his hand. Based on the worn tennis ball, the flattened place on the carpet, and the slick spot on the wall, he had been at it for a while. Disbarred lawyers apparently had lots of time on their hands.

"Won't the landlord frown upon the defacement of the office?"

"Hold on a second and let me ask. No, he does not care."

"Does that mean you own this place?"

"Got it in one. You really are an investigator."

"Whatever. But I do have a case for you." I pulled out the

dollar bill Vicky had given me. "Straight from the client. She needs help."

"I'm always here ready to help a damsel in distress."

"Not sure what damsel even means, but I believe her to be a formidable woman. Yet in a bad spot right now. You might even know her."

"And she is?"

"Vicky Vickers."

"I don't know her, but I know of her. Doyle's widow."

"Got it in one." I decided turnabout was fair play. "Somebody from Atlanta is trying to take everything she has and is blaming it on Doyle's criminal activities."

"Impossible. I drew up an estate plan for Doyle. As mean and dumb as he was, he followed it to the letter and kept his activities away from his house and property. Even his legitimate business is squeaky clean. Well, except for the trucks."

"Somebody has Vicky scared."

"Who might be the proverbial wolf at the door?"

"Pamela Foster."

Larry quit bouncing and catching the ball. Then he started laughing. "Really? This is too good."

"From that, I guess you know her."

Larry opened a file drawer and took out two folders. He put them on the desk between us.

"These two folders include the information you requested detailing Benjamin Rawley's less than savory behavior and criminal endeavors. Open the top folder."

I opened it and began reading. Very interesting and definitely illegal. Names of others were redacted in indelible black ink.

"You see those redacted names?"

"I do."

"Well, most of those redact marks reference one Pamela Foster. She is neck deep in Benjamin's deals and is the liaison between him and his slimy cronies in the statehouse."

"Oh, this is good. I love the coincidence."

"She must have gotten word about Vicky's predicament from Benjamin and thought she could swoop in and intimidate Vicky. I imagine she will be throwing out bogus threats, trying to get her to sign over most everything that was Doyle's. Pamela will probably offer to let her keep the house in order to not make any trouble over the rest of everything. Vicky will probably cave unless she has a lawyer. But Pamela would have checked and would not have approached unless she thought Vicky could not afford one."

"You seem to have knowledge of this kind of scam."

"Used to be done all over the region, especially after someone died. Further east it was done by the early kaolin companies."

"It is a good thing she now does have a lawyer. Sort of."

"True enough. But I see a fortuitous culmination of events."

"Take down both Benjamin and Pamela, while making Vicky a happy woman?"

"Exactly. She needs to get her dollar's worth."

"A plan I can believe in. Do you want Vicky to come down to your office?"

"Absolutely. Now that I'm on retainer I hope to bury Pamela once and for all."

"That sounds a little personal."

"She went to the District Attorney after my arrest and tried to talk him into sentencing me to do five years in prison. I think she knew I had a little money and was looking for a bribe."

"And now it is time for payback."

"Time and a half. If I can get her on tape lying and intimidating Vicky, then she might be looking at five years in prison. Might even back off the greedy crooks in Atlanta. Do you think Vicky will go for it?"

"I am almost certain she will."

"Since you know who has been redacted in the one file, let me give you the unredacted version. There should be more than enough for you to use to remove Benjamin from your campus."

"You know, if we time this right, then Pamela won't be able to perform her liaison duties to help Benjamin."

"That is what I'm thinking. The boys in Atlanta won't take his calls directly once Pam is gone."

"A win-win for once."

"I'm all for those, especially with these people."

"On the way back I'll stop by and tell Vicky to come see you. How much should I tell her?"

"You know her and I don't. Tell her whatever you think will convince her to play along."

"It should not take too much convincing."

"Good. Had anyone else shooting at you lately?"

"No, not even a mean glance. But I think I have an idea who it might be. I don't think it will happen again."

"Sure about that?"

"I think you just gave me what I needed to ensure it."

"Who was it?"

"They should remain anonymous until I confirm."

"A mystery then. Are you willing to bet your life on it?"

"In this case, yes."

"I'll leave you to it. I have balls to bounce."

"Give this place a quick cleanup before Vicky gets here."

"Why? I think it looks fine."

"Did I tell you how attractive Vicky is?"

"Oh, no, you did not. But in that case I will pick up the place and vacuum. Thanks for the referral."

As I left Larry's office. I momentarily wondered if I had done the right thing. If Larry and Vicky got together, they might use their powers for evil. But nah, that was unlikely to happen. Meanwhile Vicky really needed Larry to get Pamela Foster out of her life. That could also help me get Benjamin Rawley out of my life. It was time Vicky got a break, and even more fortunate for me that I had a hand in it. It would make our next conversation easier.

I got some food in Hamilton at a sandwich place and decided my next actions. I needed to give Vicky a little more time before I saw her again. I was not making much progress in the Lester case, but thought talking to Duffy was worth the effort. I decided to give Duffy a try although it was a little early in the afternoon.

Earlier I had gone through all the feathers I had brought back from Watkinsville. I needed a few to get Duffy's attention. I felt bad about using feathers to get him to talk, but I needed to know what he knew. If he even knew anything. But if something happened in the Cove, I was betting that he knew about it.

The sun was fairly near the place in the sky as the first time I had met Duffy along the road. I drove past our first meeting site and found him further up the road. He stood still as I pulled alongside him.

"Hi Duffy."

"You are James and looking for the river."

"I am. And I have feathers. You have nice carved stones."

He nodded.

"Thanks for giving me directions to the river. The other question I wanted to ask was if you know anything about those big white dishes up the road?"

"I remember when they came. People came with them and stayed there. The bowls moved around. They looked funny when they moved around. I could not get near them although I once tried. But then I didn't want to because they hummed bad. Made my ears and stomach hurt when I tried to get near them at night. One day the people all went away. Some more people came for a while, then they went away. The bad hum is not there now. I go sometimes at night."

"Why do you like to go to the bowls?"

"The bowl talks to me. It hears everything and hums it back. A good hum. I like to go there. Sometimes I sleep there when it's warm."

"What kind of hum or sound do you hear?"

"Everything you can see from the bowl speaks to it. It gathers it all up and sends it back out, but it is different. It's like the river. I go there because it whispers all the time. It talks louder where the big rocks are. The bowl speaks like that, but different. Water sounds one way, air sounds a different way."

"I've heard the river. I think I've heard the air, too. Duffy, you are a very insightful person."

"Insightful. Insightful. What does that mean?"

"Somebody that hears and sees what others do not. Being

able to do that and understanding what is around them. A lot of people can't do that, but I think you can."

"Insightful. I think I like that word. Oh yes. I'm going to keep it. Do you want a shaped stone to trade for it?"

"No thanks, Duffy. No trade, because words are freely given. Take the ones you want and ignore the rest."

"I like that, yes. Like drinking water while it moves past. I take the sips I want, but then stop. The water keeps going. You think words are like that?"

"I do. Words are sounds in the air. Take them or let them keep floating."

"I like the way you say things. I understand better."

"I thank you for your talk, Duffy. I would like for you to take another feather. Your choice."

"Yes, please, thank you. Yes please." Duffy carefully chose a mottled flight feather from a pileated woodpecker. It was a shed feather from a wild bird that Richard had taken in on trade. Duffy held it up to the sun. "The sun tells the truth. This is a good one."

"I'm glad you like it. Here, also take this turkey feather."

"I have a stone for you. It is worth two feathers." Duffy took a large stone from his pocket. It was nearly three inches long and made from white quartz so it was probably a spearhead or a scraper. Most people called everything an arrowhead. But many artifacts found were too large to have been fitted on the end of an arrow.

"Thank you Duffy. I'm going to leave now but will be back to visit my friend. I hope to see you again."

"Who are your friends?"

"Sam and Irene. They live that way about a mile. Near that nice barn but up on the hill."

"I know them a little. Nice people, they give me garden food."

"They are nice. I will see you soon. Bye."

He waved as I drove off. I had more questions for him but I didn't want to interrogate him or scare him. I thought about what he said about the bowls speaking to him. The acoustics on the dish likely did catch most sounds and possibly concentrate the sounds waves and echo them back off the dish.

CHAPTER THIRTEEN

On the way back from Athens and Watkinsville I thought I saw a familiar motorcycle outside Monticello. I saw it again when I was coming back from Larry's office in Hamilton. It was time to find out who my two-wheeled stalker was.

Each morning I had been keeping watch out of my side window in the kitchen. The telescope Millard have given me was heavy, but I had put it by the window. If my motorcycle stalker was on campus watching me, they were most likely across the field, inside the thin row of woods along the road. Not too far from where my shooter had been. It was the best place to see my house without being seen by anyone passing on the road if they were hidden. Just far enough into the woods to evade the hourly campus police patrol, but close enough to the road to watch me, then follow when I left.

The telescope was so powerful I was able to confirm something was parked there several times over the past three days.

As I stood drinking my morning coffee, I saw a flash, similar to sunlight hitting chrome or glass. My cue to jump in the old tank of a car and chase down my chaser. The rider probably though I was in for the morning and took a break to get breakfast or put gas in the bike. Motorcycles got good gas mileage but had small tanks.

I exited campus and turned right toward town. There were only two gas stations so if the bike wasn't there I'd check the other few places to eat besides Mable's. The bike was parked at the second station while the rider was filling the tank. I turned in and parked a few inches from the front tire of the bike in case the rider intended quick flight. But what I got was no reaction at all.

The rider was dressed in typical black leather bike clothing to provide maximum protection against wrecks. They wore a helmet with a dark full face shade, and they didn't acknowledge my presence. I got out and walked toward the bike. The head swiveled my direction and hands came up to the helmet. It came off to reveal a striking young woman. I was surprised and saw the smirk on her face, so she knew how her presence surprised me. Something about her seemed familiar, but I could not recall ever meeting her.

"Hey, I need to talk to you," I said.

"I can't talk to you," she said.

"Yeah you can, if you were sent by Atlanta. I told them not to send anyone, but they did, anyway."

"I'm supposed to keep you safe, not engage in conversation."

"I think it is possible to do both. As long as we are not seen together too often."

"What did you have in mind?"

"Later tonight, meet me on the back porch. Nobody will see us there."

"That is real close to the police station."

"Yes, but they leave me alone."

"OK, I'll be there at 10 pm."

"Thanks. See you then."

I backed up and left for home. The rider I had just met was probably twenty-five, with brown hair and green eyes. How she had gotten mixed up in the Atlanta mob I had no idea. Since they had sent her to check on me, she was likely quite competent. But for now I had breakfast to eat and other things to think about.

I went to the bookstore as I had been absent a lot the past few days. I took the bike in with Kat. Lottie and Millard had been keeping the store open, but I told them I wanted to get back in the rotation. I was not worried about an assassin trying to kill me any longer.

I opened the store and let Kat roam. She did her usual sniffing and rubbing on all her familiar spots. I walked around the place, enjoying the sight of all the books and the smell. A combination of new books, with the paper and ink, along with the old smell of the store. Mostly wood with a tinge of dust. The ancient wide pine floor planks creaked occasionally as I moved around. No one could sneak up on you in this place. Perhaps a carpet runner down the middle aisle would look good and reduce the noise. Something to look into.

When I got to the back of the store, I turned and looked

to the front. Something seemed to be missing. All the new books were in their places along the many shelves. But much of the store was filled with what the Big Five publishers dictated from their lists of popular authors and titles. It gave us a lot less freedom to display other books. We did have a section of classics, and another for local authors. But still, the store lacked a certain character.

I thought of the great bookstores I had visited over the years. San Francisco, Portland, New York, London, Maastricht. Then I thought about what I would want as a customer in Warm Springs. Intuition finally kicked in and I realized a funky collection of used books might round out the store. I didn't know anything about the used book market, but it was not long ago that I didn't know anything about running a bookstore either. Now I had a purpose, since Lottie and Millard easily ran the rest of the operation. I even had space in the back where I could bring in and sort used books.

Other than talking to a few customers, I spent the rest of the day planning how to convert a section of the store into used books, as well as learning something about how to find and purchase them. I'd consult with Lottie and Millard to make sure they were on board with the new idea. Then it was time to take myself and Kat home and have dinner.

I was sitting on the back porch with a pitcher of iced tea and two glasses after dark. Kat was keeping me company. There was a bottle of alcohol as well to add to the tea if she wanted it. The crickets and katydids were deep in their screaming match this time of year so I never heard her approach. All I noticed was a shadow darker than the surroundings as she stepped onto the porch. Kat tensed up but then relaxed.

"Would you like some cold tea?" I asked.

"Sure."

"I also have this if you'd like to turbocharge it."

She looked at the bottle. "No thanks. I've heard drinking liquor in your house can be hazardous." Kat proceeded to slink over and sniff the strange human. Then she stayed and purred.

"Geez, kill one guy and people get nervous. Everybody knows you can't use the same weapon twice. Iced tea, now, that is a far better conduit of certain poisons." She did not even pause as she lifted her glass and drank. "I guess you are not worried."

"No, I'm not."

"Like I said earlier today, I don't need Atlanta sending a babysitter."

"Like I said before, it doesn't matter. I'm following orders. Until you convince them otherwise and they tell me different, I'm here to swaddle and burp you and keep you from putting bad things in your mouth."

"Sounds like you have experience with babies."

"Just nephews and nieces."

We sat in the dark listening to the chorus of insects. Kat had now adopted the stranger and was accepting head and back pets. I often found silence a good way to get others to talk. Unless they were like me, in which case the silence could go on for hours.

"You know who I am, but who are you?"

"Call me Sabrina. You don't remember me, do you?"

"No, I don't."

"I saw you for the first time years ago at a funeral. I was a little girl so no reason for you to remember me. Then again about ten years ago. Another funeral, and I was a teenager."

"Maybe I do remember that. You were with two others, a boy and a girl."

"Yeah, my cousins. Or should I say, our cousins."

"Oh, I should have known. I never considered you are part of the next generation that is coming along in the business."

"Was not my first choice. But the world got tough in the past few years. Expensive, and now you can't even get a student loan for college. The business is where I found my slot. Don't look at me like that."

"Like what?"

"You are giving me that pity face look. I don't need it. I made my choice, and it is what I do now."

"If it is what you really want, then congratulations. If not, and you want to talk about alternatives, let me know."

"Thanks but no thanks. I know you got out, but you probably had better options. I'm staying where I'm at."

"Understood. Now, what have you seen or heard since you've been watching me?"

"You are a boring person."

"I can't argue with that. But I was more interested in whether you observed anyone anyone lurking around with murderous intent."

"After talking to you, I imagine you generate murderous intent from everyone around you. But no, nothing specific. Whoever was after you before, it is not happening now."

"How long are you here to watch me?"

"Indefinitely, the last I heard. Although if the shooter is caught, there would be no reason for me to stay."

"Extra incentive for you to find them."

"Or let them kill you soon. I get to go home either way."

"You have a point. But your career will be enhanced by keeping me alive."

"Are you sure about that?"

"Relatively sure."

"Then I better get back to it."

"You know you really don't have to. I'm sure the shooter wanted to warn me, not kill me."

"You can call and tell that to Atlanta. Until they tell me otherwise, you are my assignment. You must be dense since that's the third time I've had to say it."

"I like to antagonize people. Hey, a last thing. If you are watching the house, if I flick the lights on and off three times it means I need to talk, and quick. Otherwise I won't bug you."

"Corny, but I guess it makes sense. But what about in the daytime?"

"Loud screaming, two gunshots in the air, or smoke signals should work. Your preference."

"Just text me at this number." She handed me a business card. It was for a maid service in Atlanta that was probably phony.

"Thanks. The house could use a deep cleaning. More importantly, now I won't have to waste ammunition or start the grill to get your attention."

She didn't respond as she slipped off the porch. Dressed in black, I could not even see her after a few steps. Kat watched her go with her feline night vision. She seemed to like the young woman.

I considered my guardian angel. Dressed in black motorcycle leathers with a smart mouth and was a criminal from Atlanta. Oh, and a distant cousin on top of everything else. She also must watch old movies, because nobody said corny anymore. Nor did she like my humor. Then again, she had drawn the short straw and got me as a surveillance subject. I was not sure who needed sympathy, me or her. One positive was that the encounter with Sabrina had convinced me even more I was no longer in danger.

CHAPTER FOURTEEN

I was at the counter in Sam and Irene's kitchen drinking coffee with them. We had not talked recently, and I wanted to give them an update although I did not have much to tell them.

"How is your investigation into Lester going?" Irene asked.

"Slow so far. I'm trying to get to know Duffy because I think he knows something."

"You don't think he did it, do you? I could not imagine him killing Lester."

"Not at all. But I do think he knows as much or more than anybody of what goes on in the Cove, day or night."

"I don't know, he is around a lot but we have never known him to talk much," Sam said.

"I get the same, but he is starting to open up a little. Have you talked to Dunder yet?"

"I have." Sam's voice was tight and Irene was watching him.

"I'm guessing it did not go great."

"He says he had nothing to do with it, and I believe him."

"Can I talk to him?"

"You can try, but don't expect he will talk to you. He definitely won't if he knows you are looking around on our behalf."

"Then I will have to try a different approach. You say he grows lots of crops in the Cove?"

"Yes, mostly corn this season. But he grows about anything if it looks profitable on the futures reports."

"I might be able to start the conversation along those lines."

"Good luck."

"Where is the best place to find him?"

"You could try his house but he lives off the road and does not like strangers in his driveway."

"He must be on his tractor a lot."

"Yes, I'll show you the fields he is working. You might catch him there."

"If he is, I'll try to get his attention."

That is how I found myself sitting outside my car beside the road in the scant shade cast by the tall vehicle. In the distance a man drove a tractor back and forth across a large field. I had already been sitting for a while. I expected him to ignore me for a time, but then I thought he would either get mad I was watching him and he would come to run me off, or he would think my car was having trouble and he would offer assistance. A likely scenario considering how poor the cell phone service was in the Cove.

But apparently Dunder did not mind being watched, nor did he have the good samaritan gene. The tractor continued its endless journey across the far end of the field. On the positive side, the tractor was slowly moving toward the front of the field where I was. I calculated he would be near the road in another 18 hours. My strategy might not be the most efficient.

An hour later the tractor stopped at the left side of the field where a dirt lane ran from the road to the far back of the field where the treeline started. Dust signaled a beat up truck was coming up the lane toward the road. Turning on the pavement toward me, it parked a few feet behind my car. A large man with tousled hair and an ample beard got out. I stood up to greet him.

"Is it your intention to cause any trouble?" he asked.

"No, not my intention."

"Are you selling anything?"

"I don't think so."

"Then what do you want?"

"To meet you and have a conversation. The time and place dependent on your schedule. I know you are busy this time of year."

"You seem to know me but I don't know you."

"I am James Wilder. I have the bookstore in Warm Springs."

"But that is not what you are known for in the county."

"I don't know how people know me."

"You are known around here because some have tried to kill you, but so far they have ended up dead or in jail."

"I guess that is fair."

"It is." He looked up at the sun. "We can have a conversation right now. The tractor needs a break."

"I appreciate it. Would you like some iced tea?"

"Do you make good tea? If so, I would gladly accept a drink. As long as it isn't poisoned."

"It is good tea. It is not poisoned as I only put poison in whiskey."

"I'll remember that if you ever offer me a whiskey sour."

"You won't be surprised to learn nobody in town wants me to pour them a drink."

"I imagine not. But that guy had it coming."

"He did. I really never felt guilty about it either."

"You got the crooked sheriff put away too."

"He did all the hard work for me. I just had to point out a few things to the right people."

"Was it you or the sheriff that got Doyle killed?"

"Once again, Doyle did all the work. The deputies killed him at the sheriff's order."

"And you are kin to Sam and Irene."

"Sort of. They are my deceased wife's cousins. I suppose they are the closest thing I have to family in this state. For not knowing me, you know a lot about me."

"I try to keep up with current events. Sorry about your wife."

"Thanks, but it has been a while."

"You want to talk about Lester, is that right?"

"Not really. I've heard a lot of stories about him. All bad."

"They are all true. But I did not kill Lester. I know Sam did not either. We both had reason to at one time. Even talked about it. But that time came and went. I assume you are looking into Lester's death to give Sam an alibi. Not that he needs one."

"That is what got me started on this quest. I think finding out more about the Cove is another reason. As part of that, I would like to ask you about Duffy."

"You need to leave him alone. He is special, and the Cove protects their own."

"Not my intention to hurt him. I just met him recently and I agree he is special. You said the Cove takes care of him. I'm glad to hear it. I was worried he was alone."

"He is, because he wants to be. But everyone out here keeps a watch on him. He does not want for anything."

"Good. Maybe I do have one question about Lester. What was his relationship with people in the Cove? I guess I'm asking if he came out a lot and if people hated him."

"It is complicated. He did have a few connections out here in the past. But he used up all of them in one way or another. Eventually he was not welcome."

"I know he came from a wealthy family and had connections in Woodbury and Hamilton County."

"Then you might be wondering what a guy like him would be doing out slumming in the Cove."

"Not exactly my words, but yeah, why was a spoiled rich kid hanging around?"

"That will be a conversation for another time. I have to get finished. Thanks for the tea, it was good." He handed me the clear plastic cup.

"Thanks for your time. Are you willing to talk to me again?"

He reached into his pocket and handed me a business card. "I'll trade you. You tell me about the poison bottle and how you got Joe to drink it, and I'll tell you about Lester and the Cove."

"You ever get lunch at Mable's?"

"Sometimes. Call me and we can meet there."

He turned around and got in his truck. I got in mine and drove home. I believed Sam. Dunder gave no indication whatever he killed Lester. But he knew something, or knew about something. Lester was not visiting the Cove just for the scenery.

Once on campus I drove by the garden. Everything looked fine. I was still bothered by what might be underneath it. But until I got word from the archaeology crew on the Flint River, there was not much I could do about it.

At home I fed myself, and more importantly, Kat. She was flexible to a point, but depriving her of dinner was not a good idea. Otherwise I would wake up in the night with her lying on my chest and raking her claws lightly on my face. It was sufficient warning that I'd get up and attend to her. Otherwise the light clawing could progress to something more aggressive, which I'm sure she knew that I knew.

I called Dunder and set up to meet him for lunch the next day. The rest of the evening passed uneventfully.

Dunder was waiting outside for me when I pulled up to Mable's. Inside, people seemed to know him and gave him nods of acknowledgment, which he returned. But there were no shaking of hands or smiling with verbal greetings. They knew who he was and were respectful but not friendly. I didn't know whether they were reacting to Dunder personally or because he represented the Cove. We sat at a smaller table and waited for Lottie.

"How much do you know about Cove history?" he asked.

"I've read a few things. But not much official history exists that I've found. Stories I've heard seem to mimic stories told about us mountain people up in the far coves and hollers in the Appalachians."

"That is appropriate. Hard people in isolated areas tend to do things to survive most other people would not."

"Also, when I tell people around here I'm going to the Cove, I get a look. Then sometimes I'm told to be careful and not go alone. People still are afraid of the place."

"They have had reason to be afraid in the past. Not anymore, but traditions persist. Just like in your deep mountains, the only law and justice were what the people there decided it was."

"Sounds familiar."

"I heard stories from my grandparents about how the Cove was a place for the dispossessed. People trickled in and most eventually left. Creek Indians, escaped slaves, and soldiers deserting from their armies all came through the Cove to hide on their way to somewhere else. After that came the resident moonshiners. The outside law, what little was around, was not welcome in the Cove. We watched our own backs and made unwelcome the strangers that came through."

"I've heard the same stories in the mountains. The only difference is the Indians were Cherokee instead of Creek."

"It is not surprising, people are people."

"I'd like to go back to our previous conversation. What was Lester doing out there a long time ago?"

"After lunch we will cross the street and sit on the bench in the shade. I'll tell you what I know and you tell me your story."

Lottie came over to take our order. "Look at this," she said. "East trouble meets West trouble, right here at lunch. I predict the earth will split open and the sky will rain cats and dogs."

"Miss Lottie, I see you have not lost your penchant for hyperbole," Dunder said.

"Don't go using your education on me young man. I used those words before you were born and gave up on them once I realized they detract from plain talk."

"Yes ma'am. I'll talk straight."

"See that you do. Besides, James here may not know any big words and get confused."

"Thanks for your confidence, Lottie," I said.

"See Dunder, that is how you get under his skin with plain words."

"I'll remember, Miss Lottie."

We ordered and Madam Gadfly left us alone.

"Where did you go to school?" I asked.

"I assume you mean for university. I was at Vanderbilt for my undergraduate studies, then to Cornell for a Master's degree. But it was too cold up there, so I came back when I finished."

"Did you plan to leave the Cove?"

"I did. But I missed it after I left. I decided to come back and farm for two years and then decide what to do. I never seemed to be able to get away after that. Although I certainly thought about it. My compromise is to take a long trip once a year."

"Where do you go?"

"I used to go to places to learn about farming techniques. China, Thailand, Sweden, India, Brazil. But I got tired of that. I now go either to the UK or northern Europe to ride the trains and visit villages. It is relaxing and an easy way to meet people."

"Do you go by yourself?"

"Sometimes. I offer to take anyone else that wants to go. I believe travel is necessary to understand the world better. Also to get a better perspective on yourself."

"I'd agree to both points."

"You were in Europe for a while. One of the bounces you made between universities and big companies until you left your career and moved here."

"Then you know a lot about my background."

"I do. That is why I told you about me. It is a small thing, but can form a basis for understanding."

"It is a good start."

Lottie brought our food but was unusually quiet. I think she understood we were having a serious conversation and left us to it. We finished, paid, and walked across the street to the benches under the shade.

CHAPTER FIFTEEN

Sitting on the bench in downtown Warm Springs, with our to-go cups of iced tea, I was reminded of the fictional town of Mayberry. My adopted town seemed to mimic the television version of America.

"James, tell me your story," Dunder said.

"I had been looking into a few people, three to be exact, for Tammy's murder. My gut was telling me that Joe, her partner, did it. I called him and threatened him with black-mail. I knew he would come over and probably try to kill me. I was walking across the living room to grab my gun when he came in my door, pointing a pistol at me. He had been right around the corner when I called instead of fifteen minutes away."

"How did he get in?"

"I had given him the pass code when I was setting him up,

pretending to sell my house. I thought he might use it to surprise me, at which point I'd surprise him."

"Didn't work out, did it?"

"No, your foe tends to not follow your plans. He came in and was going to shoot me in the head and make it look like a suicide. Then he saw the bottle of whiskey and realized it was worth more than my car. He decided to have a drink and I let him."

"You were lucky."

"Oh yes. Now I'm here and Joe is in the ground. I think he was surprised."

"I imagine so."

"I'm just trying to figure out why a man buys a bottle for what, twelve thousand dollars, then adds poison and keeps it on the shelf."

"It was a little more than twelve. Have you ever seen a bad cancer take a loved one, up close and personal?"

"I have not."

"Good. The bottle was my out, especially if I was diagnosed with a bad one."

"Understood. Ironic, and fortunate for keeping you alive instead of Joe."

"It served its purpose, just not in a way I had ever imagined."

"Life tends to be that way. Then you got tangled up with Doyle Vickers and Sheriff Jackson."

"Not by choice. Bryan got me into it by looking at the Mike Vickers murder. Then Doyle and the sheriff mostly took care of getting themselves dead or in jail. How well did you know them?"

"Not well, fortunately. Doyle was Doyle. Mean and ugly

but everyone knew what to expect. The sheriff, now, he was mean and ugly too, but much worse because he was smarter. Smart enough to get elected and shield himself from most of his crimes. That made him more dangerous than Doyle. I'm glad the sheriff is gone away."

"Me too."

"Now I suppose you would like to hear about Lester."

"I would. I don't think Lester's body ended up back in the Cove by accident."

"I don't think so either. Before I begin, I assume you know something about his past, how he grew up in wealth in Woodbury?"

"Some of it."

"His parents had ridden the wave of pimento farming and canning. They made a lot of money. And a lot of money in the 1960s Woodbury was a huge amount of money."

"I can only imagine. The top 1% of the most wealthy in a small town."

"Lester knew that life, but always wanted more even as a teenager. Although he was clever enough, and could talk anybody into anything, he was not actually good at anything. Whether managing the fields or supervising the canning plant, nothing lasted more than a few months. Eventually he ended up at the Savings and Loan due to his family connections. That position allowed him to wield influence and amplify his grifter nature across the county.

"Without going into details, I came from a family of farmers and moonshiners. From that I knew how to grow things and how to run an illegal business. Sam and Irene came into the picture about that time and we were able to set up a venture. Lester was shrewd enough to know what we were doing and offered his services to launder money. Despite my better judgement, we agreed. But I never trusted him so he only ever got a part of my money. I'm sure Sam and Irene could tell you more.

"But back to the original topic. Lester came out to the Cove for reasons of his own. Maybe he wanted to be the rich boy gone rogue. A bad boy. Or maybe by then everyone in Woodbury and most of Hamilton County had seen through him, so he went to the Cove to look for more marks. I think that is how he saw everyone other than himself. He spent money and bought liquor to gain favor. Then he foreclosed on a house after the owner died, which lost him some of the goodwill his money had bought him. He moved a girlfriend in the house but that lasted only a few months. After fixing a few things he sold it to a family, then kicked them out because he had rigged the contract. Not much later he quit coming to the Cove. From what I've heard more than one party threatened him harm if he came back. The abandoned house eventually deteriorated and nothing is left but some of the foundation and chimney.

"After that, another young woman seemed to like Lester, at least a little. She did not come from a great family and she was on her own by the time she was 18. Her grandparents left her their place since the girl's mother was their only daughter. The mother had married badly, and the husband went to jail. The mother left with another man and never came back, nor did the father when he got out of jail. The house went to the girl by default."

"The young woman was Duffy's mom?"

"That is the story. Probably not worth the effort to prove it."

"How many of the stories do you think are true? I'm not saying I don't believe them, I just would like to know how complicated Lester's life was in the Cove."

"I'd guess the stories are 80% true. I'm sure a lot of details got left out. Maybe a few things were added."

"It fits the pattern of what I've heard about Lester from other people around the county."

"He was consistent in his bad behavior."

"Does Duffy know anything about the Lester rumors?"

"No, I don't think anyone told him. You can see why."

"Yeah, having Lester as a father is not a positive. Do you know other stories about Lester and the Cove? I'd like to have as much about his activities out there as possible. Not trying to get anyone in trouble, just fleshing out Lester."

"I don't know any more. I can ask a few people that were around during that time. They may or may not talk."

"Good enough. I'm still curious about Duffy."

"He's different but a good soul."

"You said people are looking after him."

"He does not need much looking after. I keep an eye on him. I take a box of groceries, mostly farm stuff, over each week. I'm not the only one. He grows stuff on his own, and he cuts his own firewood for heating and cooking. Folks around here all know him. If he needs a pair of boots, clothes, or a coat, it gets left at his place."

"I'm glad to hear it. What about electricity, indoor plumbing, that kind of thing?"

"He stays at his mom's old place. He is kind of genius when it comes to some things. He rigged up a system to generate electricity from the stream that falls down the hill behind the house. Charges the batteries he has collected, so he has enough electricity for lights and a radio. Also keeps the well pump going. He heats water with another rig he put together that looks almost like a copper still attached to the wood stove. About the only things he does not have are a television or a computer."

"He does not have much entertainment options out there."

"The library sets up a lending box, which happens to be near his place in the Cove. From what I've heard he reads several books a week."

"That is amazing. He is living off-grid, mostly self-sufficient, and seems to be fine."

"Like I said, we keep an eye on him. If we don't see him for a day or two one of us will go to his house. If he is sick, he gets a ride to the doctor in Woodbury."

"I appreciate the talk today, Dunder."

"What are you going to do with it?"

"I'm not sure. I am not any closer to figuring out who killed Lester, although that might not be important."

"Nor healthy considering how much he was hated."

"True. I'll also keep some feathers in the car for Duffy. He seems to like them and when I see him, I'll stop and say hello."

"He does like his feathers. But you know he won't make a good witness."

"No, there is no chance he would. Nor would I ever put him in that position. Possibly he saw or heard something that might help, but I'd take that on myself."

"Good. You seem to know your limits. You know the Cove will have have a problem with you should you try to force Duffy into anything."

"I understand, and that won't be a problem."

Something Duffy said about the dish resonated with me. Both from a witness perspective and from an aesthetic viewpoint. How much could he have seen happening from the dish he was in pointed to the west? I also wanted to experience sitting in the dish to determine if there were sounds or vibrations the dish picked up or concentrated.

The police were done with the area and somebody had cleaned off the bloody word. But it was still private property, and the gate was locked when I got there. I parked in a grown up lane a hundred yards past the dish complex. I walked back to the tall fence and decided not to climb it. Duffy seemed to come here often, and he must have an easier way in.

I went left from the gate by the road to the field side to check the perimeter. It was easy at first as it was an overgrown field but no weeds more than waist-high. But soon I ran into a vast kudzu patch. I had no intention of wading into that mess that was twenty feet high in some places. The snakes and ticks would have to wait for someone else to come along.

Back at the gate I went, then around the right side. It was thick at first but quickly turned into scrubby woods with only a few briars. I picked up what I thought was a deer trail and followed it just feet from the tall fence. When the trail veered off downhill away from the fence, I moved toward it and saw a cut in the chain links. It had been partially spliced back together but only took me a few seconds to unzip it.

I squeezed through and followed a narrow trail in tall grass and young pines about twenty feet tall. They blocked my view but moments later I saw the west dish towering above me. The trail took me to a concrete structure that reminded me of an old, large, water reservoir. But it was the base of the dish. I followed the circular structure and found a metal ladder embedded in the concrete. I scaled it and was quickly on top of the concrete and under the base of the metal superstructure of the dish. A short flight of metal steps with paint flaking off led up to an initial platform, then a steep set of steps ended on a large platform with an enclosed metal room taking up most of the space. I walked around it but the one door was locked.

I assumed either the electrical panels, motors, or the giant gears that moved the dish were in the room. I found a metal ladder built into the external wall and climbed up as there was no other way to ascend. Atop the metal room, a second long ladder led up through the heavy metal supports directly under the dish. It was a tight fit, but I made it up and found a small hatch partially open, and could see the sky beyond. Pushing through it gave me access to the surface of the dish. I also realized why Lester's body had to be brought up by ladder to the lip of the dish. There was no way to carry a body up the way I had just traversed.

I took a moment and oriented myself. I had an image of stepping onto the dish and sliding off it and dropping thirty feet to the ground. At my age I probably would not recover. But I realized the angle of the dish was close to flat between me and the edge, although curve of the dish to either side did get steep and go up quickly. The surface of the dish was in rough shape so I did not have to worry about slipping.

I still stayed on all fours as I moved away from the center. I stopped a few feet from the edge and sat to study my surroundings. A nice view of the countryside before me for a few miles to the edge of the crater, while behind me and towering up nearly a hundred feet was the off-white bowl. I listened to the sounds of the late-season grasshoppers in the grass below, along with a few birds in the low pines.

It was peaceful and a nice view. The setting was disorienting at first with the curvature of the dish but I was adjusting. As a breeze came through I heard, or maybe felt, a slight hum. With all the superstructure below holding up the dish, the vibration was odd but not unexpected. When the dish was active years ago, they must have had a way to dampen the vibration, or perhaps it did not affect the signal they were searching for.

I moved back toward the center of the dish. The vibration lessened, yet it seemed the noise of the bugs and birds changed. Louder but somehow deeper and lower, probably changed by the acoustics of the dish bouncing sound around in different patterns and resonating across the surface. This must be what Duffy heard when he was on the dish. I moved back toward the lip of the dish and heard the same sounds as before, but they sounded more natural.

I sat and slowly moved closer the very edge. I could the other dish from the back, and a little of one side. If Duffy sat here, he would have been able to see a truck pull up, lift up a ladder or bucket, but would not have seen what happened inside the dish. And this was in the daytime, not at night. I sat longer and watched the sun go lower. I didn't know how it felt to be here at night and did not want to stay. But I needed to know what Duffy could have seen at night.

The long Georgia twilight began and the grasshopper noise diminished while the bird noise increased. The light turned more golden, then orange. Finally the sun was down, and the birds quieted as the crickets and last of the katydids began their singing. As the sky darkened, it seemed the dishes began to glow. It was a trick of the mass of white paint reflecting the light. Even as the night deepened, the glow remained. Duffy could have seen what was happening a lot better than I thought.

Before it got any later I needed to get off the dish. I strapped on a headlight and backtracked my steps across the dish, and down the ladder and steps. Instead of skirting around through the fields and trees to go back through the fence, I went straight to the locked gate and scaled it. An easy walk back to my vehicle.

I had also been counting cars since dark. Six cars total, early in the evening. Probably none after midnight or later, when the body was placed. Likely nobody but Duffy witnessed the event. Even if someone had driven by, a truck parked under the dish with no lights on it would have gone unnoticed. I needed more conversation with Duffy as he was the only witness. If he was not here that night, the investigation was going to be a lot harder.

CHAPTER SIXTEEN

I invited Vicky over to campus for a quick lunch at the cafeteria. I was trying to keep things casual and in public spaces. People might talk but I was not concerned. Most of the people closest to me were aware nothing was going on between me and Vicky. I had her meet me at my house and park there before we walked to lunch.

When she got out of the car, I saw her flash a big smile, then watched as it turned into a sad scowl. Then back to a small smile.

"James, I'm glad to see you."

"Are you sure?"

"Yes, I am. I met with Larry in Hamilton. I finally think things are about to get better. Thank you so much for putting us together."

"Larry can get things right for you. I'm glad it worked out."

"It is not done yet. I still have to put on a performance and get the woman on tape. But that will be easy. She thinks she is going to bully me into giving her everything. All I have to do is act like I'm going to cry and beg for mercy."

"I don't know if Larry told you, but this also helps me out."

"He said Pamela was involved in campus business and you would like her gone as well."

"I would. Well, not gone necessarily, but gone enough to quit protecting my ongoing thorn."

Then we walked to lunch and made small talk. After we ate, we walked back to my house.

"James, thanks again for lunch. And putting me together with Larry."

"You are welcome. But before you go, I think we need to talk."

"We do?"

"I believe it is time to clear up something. Vicky, I understand you are, or were, quite a deer hunter."

"I am, or I guess I was. My father took me hunting and taught me how. I grew up around it, even though most girls my age did not hunt."

"What rifle do you prefer?"

"I have used several. Why?"

"I used to shoot an odd caliber, a .356, in a lever action. Good for reasonable distances, great for brush. I'm guessing you are more of a .270 caliber shooter. Bolt action most likely."

"James, why are you asking me about this?"

"I think you know. I certainly do. Not that I'm going to do anything about it."

"James..."

"Yes, Vicky?"

"I can't say it. I just can't. I want to tell you. I want to make it up to you. But I can't."

"Let me help you. For reasons you have yet to tell me, you did something. Then you felt bad about it and have been trying to make it up to me. I appreciate it, but now we need to talk about what happened and why. You will feel better once it is out. And you won't continue to be acting like the guiltiest person in the county."

"You have been so nice to me. And I was so mean to you."

"Tell me what you did. Then tell me why."

"I came here to the campus. I was so mad, and so broken up. Pamela Foster had just left my house telling me she was taking everything. I remembered what you told me about me getting what I wanted from the divorce and more if Doyle was gone. When Pamela left, I blamed you. I thought you had put her up to it. I was not thinking right, and I was going crazy."

"I understand. Doyle was not around to blame. Nor the sheriff since he was in jail. I can see why I was on the list. If nothing else, because I had been involved, and I was still walking around."

"I can't defend myself. Only that I was out of my mind and acting crazy."

"Crazy enough to bring your rifle to campus. Enough to shoot at me. Yet you, a dead sharpshooter, missed me by three feet."

"James, I am so sorry. I didn't adjust the scope enough

and hit your car. I never meant for that to happen. Shooting that close to someone goes against everything I was ever taught. I was shaking when I pulled the trigger. I was not even going to shoot the gun. Before you got home, I waited for a half hour, talking myself out of it. Then when I was about to leave I saw you in front of the house. I got upset again, and told myself one shot in the tree would scare you and make me feel better."

"Did it work?"

"No, I've felt awful ever since. Worse than before. I was ready to give in to Pamela because I thought I deserved to lose everything for being so stupid. James, I'll go to Bryan and tell him what I did."

"Absolutely not. And don't ever tell anyone else about it either."

"What?"

"It's over. I'm not pressing charges or telling Bryan. You need to quit worrying about it, and get on with your life. But I do have one question."

"What?"

"Why the second shot?"

"I was so messed up I chambered the second round out of reflex. I panicked and just shot the tree. It was so stupid and so dangerous. It could have ricocheted off the tree and hit something or somebody."

"Probably not your best moment."

"It was not. The past days I have not been sleeping or eating much. I ate more of your food that night than I had eaten since the shooting. James. I will never do that again."

"I hope not. But like I said, now it is over."

"No, not yet. I'm going to pay for your car."

"Will that make you feel better?

"Yes, please let me."

"I don't know, you need to save up to pay Larry's bill."

"He said you had already paid him. I didn't understand that either. Why would you do that?"

"You remember that dollar you gave me?"

"Yes."

"That was Larry's payment. It is an old joke you will have to ask him about sometime."

"I'll ask him tomorrow night. We are having dinner."

"Great. You should have your appetite back."

She smiled. "Maybe. We have to plan for Pamela. She will be back in a few days."

"Good, I hope it works out for you and me."

"James, thank you. I mean it."

"Shoot a deer this year and donate to the food bank in my name."

"I can't."

"Why not?"

"I was so messed up I threw that gun in the Flint River. I don't think I'll ever pull a trigger again. I get sick just thinking about it."

"Now you can stop worrying so much. The shooting thing is over, Doyle is gone, and Larry is about to make Pamela go away. Your life should be getting better real soon."

"I can't thank you enough."

"Maybe you can help me with something else."

"What?"

"When Mike Vickers was killed, Doyle drove his truck to dump the body."

"Yes I remember. There was some kind of video proving it."

"That's right. Poor quality but it showed Doyle's truck for sure, along with someone that looked like Doyle driving. But the tape was sent in for further analysis. It showed there was a passenger in the truck."

"Surely you don't think I was in the truck?"

"No, I don't. But you knew Doyle and who he hung out with. Would any of his guys been involved with that?"

"No, none if his drivers or guys at the shop. They knew nothing of his crooked stuff. He did not trust them enough to tell them anything, much less involve them."

"Do you think it could have been Sheriff Jackson? He seemed to be involved with Mike's murder."

"No, I don't think so. He was smart enough to never be in the wrong place with any witnesses. But if it was anyone from that crew of goons, it was his deputy, Deacon."

"Why do you say that?"

"Any time the sheriff needed something nasty done, Doyle said Deacon would do it. He handled all the sheriff's ugly business. So if the sheriff was involved with Mike's murder, he would have sent Deacon to deal with it."

"That is good to know. The sheriff brought him along to the bookstore one day to trash it and arrest me, but it did not go as planned."

"It was not a fluke that Deacon was with him. You are lucky it did not happen. He is dangerous."

"Thanks Vicky for telling me about Deacon."

"I'm glad he is in jail."

"Me too."

"James, thanks again for everything." She hugged me.

More like a bear hug. Then she released and stepped back. "I won't forget what you've done for me."

"You are welcome." I didn't know what that meant but maybe it would turn into something good. But at least Vicky would not be acting so unusual and showing up at my house anymore.

I decided a campus walk was due me. The fall flowers were coming along, especially the yellow goldenrod and the blue asters. The small clusters of thyme were still blooming pale pink as well.

On the far side of the loop I saw Millard on the porch. He waved me up. I noticed the vest of the day was green with yellow florals and tiny red and blue flowers. I thought it was too spring-like for the season but did not point it out. Then again, I had just seen fall flowers that mimicked some of the vest's colors. So much for my fashion sense.

"You are looking chipper today," Millard said. "Did Donna take you back?"

"Not at all. We are taking even more of a break than before. But I did get something over with that has been bothering me."

"What is that?"

"I found out who shot me and resolved the issue," I said.

"Who? We need to know to assign a winner."

"It does not matter. We have resolved our differences. But let me see your bingo card."

"What?"

"You know, the matrix you have, with all the suspects on it for the betting pool."

"Give me a minute, I'll print it."

Two minutes later he handed it to me and I studied it. No Vicky Vickers was listed.

"Sorry, Millard, no hits. Nobody won gunshot bingo."

"That can't be right. It is nearly impossible. We have everybody on here that does not like you."

"What can I say, you missed one. I'm global in my disfavor, I guess."

"I don't get it. The list was as comprehensive as it could be. You really must have cut a wide swath of dislike in your short time here. Wait, was it someone from your former life, or somebody from out of the county?"

"Nope, neither."

"This will dishearten the gang."

"Oh, I don't know. Maybe make this a long-term pool with big stakes. When the name finally comes out, somebody could win big."

"You know, that might work. The downside is several of us might be dead before then."

"Just make sure you outlast them. You'll win the pot by attrition even if you don't have money on the right names."

"I like the way you think. Reminds me to schedule my checkup at the doctor. This new doctor is quite attractive. I really enjoyed lunch."

"Be careful, Lottie will cancel your check if she catches you looking too much."

"No she won't, she will just laugh. As an older woman she knows better than anybody the doctor has no interest in me."

"True enough."

"You, however, might have a shot."

"I don't because I won't even try. Just not my interest right now. Not that she would even be receptive."

"James, you need to chase happiness while you can. Soon enough you'll get a bum hip and not be able to anymore."

"That's OK. Besides, you found Lottie long after your hip went bum."

"I guess. Say, any progress on Lester's murder?"

"Not really. Too many suspects."

"I know what you mean. We put up a suspect matrix, and it is several times larger than your suspect list. Maybe you'll feel good knowing Lester was more hated than you. Of course, he had about a 70 year head start on you. You have done well picking up enemies considering how short a time you've been in town."

"Thanks."

CHAPTER SEVENTEEN

It was another bright fall day with blue skies. I went to Mable's for lunch. I was not hungry but wanted to check the seasonal menu. If nothing else I could get a pastry and a coffee. But my real reason to visit was to see Lottie.

"Lottie, is there anyone in the county left from Lester's family, or an old friend?"

"Not much of either. He used up all his friends over the years, along with his ex-wives. Better you don't even try to talk to any of those women. They'd rather shoot you than talk about him. I think I remember a cousin still alive. I'll go in the back and check my computer."

"Thanks."

I continued with lunch. The past couple of weeks, even when I had been in Mable's, my time was spent working on my or Lester's case. It was nice to have a little excitement in

Warm Springs, but lately it had been too much. I needed to get back to a quieter life.

"The only family of record left is a cousin," Lottie said when she came back. "She lives in Woodbury in one of the nice older homes. A widow. She probably won't talk to you because she, just like everyone else, quit having anything to do with Lester a long time back. Her name is Margaret and I've written down her address if you still want to talk to her."

"Thanks. It might be worth a conversation. All she can do is refuse to talk to me."

Twenty minutes later I was at the address. A large house with light yellow siding, two story, with large working blue shutters. The house sat on an oversized lot with massive oak trees in the yard, and possibly pecan trees in the back. The foundation and front porch were surrounded with old azalea bushes that must make quite a show in the spring. It was a nice place like the homes often found in small Southern towns. I knocked on the ornate wooden from door.

A smaller, older woman opened the door partway. "Yes?" she asked.

"Hello, my name is James Wilder. I'm from Warm Springs and have the bookstore there."

"I have not been over yet," she said. "Do I know you?"

"I don't think so. I came by to talk about one of your relatives, if you are willing?"

"Who?"

"Lester Owens."

"I'm not sure I want to talk about him."

"I think you might be his last relative, even though distant."

"I have not let on to anyone that I'm related to him in

years. A few people remember of course. Why do you want to know about him?"

"Besides having the bookstore, I'm also a writer. After everything I've heard about him, he seems to make a colorful character. Not that I'd use him or his name directly, but would fictionalize it somewhat."

"Would this character be a hero or a villain in your book?"

"I'm afraid from everything I have heard, there is no way to make that character a hero. Just the opposite. A villain."

"Then come in, Mr. Wilder. Let's have some tea and a chat."

"Thanks."

We sat in her parlor or front study. All the furniture was old oak wood with patterns of upholstery. It was a quintessential grandmother's home. Margaret brought both of us a glass of iced tea. She was the epitome of the local church lady. Nice, polite, and probably had a machete behind the sofa for bothersome people like me.

"I appreciate you speaking to me," I said. "I was not sure of the reception I would get when I asked about Lester."

"Then you already know something about him."

"Just general comments and a few stories of things he did and people he wronged."

"To start at the beginning, Lester was a cousin, a second cousin. We played together when we were children. Woodbury was small and the family often got together after church. We drifted apart as we got older. By the time we were grown I realized I didn't like him. The past 40 and more years I did not let on to people that we were kin nor did I seek his company. A few weddings and several funerals were events where I saw him. More recently I might see him once a year at the store or the county fair.

"Even though I was taught not to speak ill of the dead, my cousin was a bad man. It was not because of his upbringing. His parents were good people, if a little greedy on the business side. But they also helped the community back when the pepper business was good. Lester grew up in a nice house and had the best of everything."

"Would that have spoiled him somewhat?"

"Perhaps. But lots of spoiled children go on to grow out of it and be good people. Lester went the other direction. It seemed every time he got something, he did not value it and only wanted more. But he learned to talk slick as he got older. I guess that is how he got his more after his parents were not around to give him things."

"A lot of people I've talked to knew him, or about him, but he did not seem to have many friends or a lasting relationship."

"No way he could have. Those closest to him got hurt the most. It is not that he was plumb mean like a mad dog. More like he was likable at first, but the longer he went on with you the more you got used. Eventually there was nothing left of you but a husk, either emotionally or financially. Then he would go and latch onto someone else. He was like a cross between a con artist and a vampire."

"That does not paint a very nice picture."

"No, it does not. Frankly, I'm surprised it took so long for him to come to a bad end."

"Was there anyone in the county that stayed close with Lester for a long time?"

"Not that I know of. All he had left at the end was his

house and cars. I know he loved his cars. He told me once that he put those antitheft little things on all of them because he was afraid somebody would steal them."

"I suppose the cars could not leave him."

"That is an apt phrase. Nor his house. But I don't know how he kept even those because he had to have been out of money. Unless he had some illegal cash somewhere."

"I heard a rumor he might have a child out in the Cove."

"It is possible. At one time he was out there a lot. He even had a house there, but it got sold. More than once from what I heard. He also probably had other children from other places scattered around. That might be where some of his money went. He would have needed to keep things quiet in this small of a town."

"Do you have any idea if where he was found was connected to anything he did before his death? I can't come up with a good reason for him to be up in that dish."

"Public humiliation is my thought. Whoever killed him wanted to show what happens to people like Lester. Can't say as I'm against it either. A fitting end for the life he led."

"What you are telling me is he had lots of enemies, and had them for a long time. The problem is the suspect list might be a couple thousand people."

"Perhaps more. And you should think about what you have to gain by finding the killer. That could make you the least popular person in the county. That is how bad the taste is in most people's mouths when it came to my cousin. I believe you are looking into the crime, not just preparing a fictional book character."

"I am interested in him as a character, but also looking into his death. But if it was not for trying to solve an associated issue that affects someone I know, I would not have any interest in looking for Lester's killer. Even so, I might not pursue it very vigorously."

"Take your own advice. Nothing good will come from it. Especially if it is someone upstanding in the community that was wronged by Lester. Sorry, but that is just how it is around here."

"I understand. Did Lester ever do anything particularly evil that you might have heard about?"

"What do you mean?"

"Did anyone near him ever go missing, for example?"

"Let me think. No, nobody went missing. If you think he was a serial killer, he was not. The only thing that went missing around him was money and a woman's virtue, if you know what I mean."

"I think I do. I appreciate you talking to me, despite the sour subject."

"That is alright, Mr. Wilder. Now do yourself a favor and leave Lester and his complications behind. They will do you no good."

"Thanks for the advice and the tea."

I left Miss Margaret's house in Woodbury and drove back out to the Cove. I was missing something but had no idea what yet. One thing I was not missing was the overwhelming dislike everyone had for Lester.

Cove Road took me up the outside of the crater, over the crest, then down into the Cove. Soon I saw Duffy pushing his empty grocery cart down the road. I parked across the road and ahead of him so he could see it was me and decide if he wanted to engage. He left his cart on the shoulder and walked over.

"Hello Duffy."

"Hi Mr. James."

"I have a new blue speckled feather if you would like to see it?"

"Oh yes, yes, I would please."

I removed the feather from a plastic protective sheet. "You have probably seen these and already have some."

"Oh yes, yes. A bluejay feather. This is a nice one."

"I also have another you might like. It is from a special breed of chicken." The feather was from a silkie, a breed of chicken that looked like a fluff ball. The base of the feather looked normal, but the outer and upper portions puffed out like a bad hair day. It was a silver color.

"Oh, I like this one. It has the down on the outside."

"That is a good description."

"Here, take this. It is from my corn field." Duffy handed me a brown rock chipped on one side to a sharp edge, and the other side was flat, dull and thick. It was probably a scraper. The dull side was gripped in the hand or fingers and the sharp side would cut or scrape anything from plant material to animal skin.

"Thanks, Duffy." I decided to get out of the car and enjoy the nice day. "I went up to the big dish the other evening. It was nice and I could hear the sounds it made."

"I like the sounds. I hear them but also feel the sounds."

"I did too. The whole thing has a hum."

"Did you sleep on it?"

"No, I didn't stay that long. I think it would be nice if the weather is good."

"It is nice. I sometimes stay if there is no thunder in the night."

"Duffy, were you up there a while back, the night before the man was found?"

"Yes, yes I was up there. The night was nice."

"That was the night somebody came out to the dish. Probably in a large truck."

"Maybe."

"I imagine you were scared. You probably thought somebody was going to tell you to leave."

"I did."

"But I bet they never even saw you. The other dish is a good place to stay out of sight."

"It is. I felt safe up there."

"Nobody saw you, but did you see anything from your dish?"

"I saw a big black locomotor. A lot bigger than your brown locomotor."

"A big and black locomotive engine?"

"Yes, but it had the other smell. The other one besides yours. Your smells like burned toast and dirt, like most around here. The other smell is bad fruit and rotten water. Lots of the biggest locomotors smell like that."

"Thanks for telling me. Was there anything else you remember about the big black locomotive?"

"Only that it was inside out."

"How is that?"

"The train track was on the inside. It is supposed to be on the outside. It was strange looking."

"Sounds interesting. I am glad nobody saw you there, and it is your secret. You can keep going to the dish and enjoy the nights."

"I like it there. It hums me to sleep."

"I am going to go back home now. Thanks for this." I held up the scraper he had traded me.

"Oh yes, thank you for the feathers."

Driving back to Warm Springs, I thought about what Duffy told me. I had other questions about what he saw that night, but decided to ask him a little at a time. I did not want to scare him or make him feel like he had done anything wrong.

If my Landcruiser was a brown locomotor, then a large black locomotor had to be a large truck. If the smell he was referring to was the exhaust, and my vehicle was gas, that meant the big black truck was a diesel. Still not a lot, but it would definitely narrow down possibilities.

The bookstore in Warm Springs was open, so I parked to see Lottie. It was her day at the store, and a break from a shift at Mable's next door.

"Hi Lottie."

"Hey James."

"What, no nickname today?"

"You have not solved any crimes lately and you don't have a girlfriend. Nor that much of a life that I can tell. What do I have left, cat dad?"

"Ouch, that is harsh. I will do something soon so you can come up with a good name."

"See that you do. Get anything good from Lester's cousin?"

"Mostly that he was a lousy person."

"A lamppost in Woodbury could have told you that."

"I do have an idea for the store."

"Let's hear it."

"I'm thinking about a used book section in the back.

Maybe something more eclectic, possibly even some of the classics."

"You must be as tired of the bestseller drivel as I am."

"Exactly. We need something better. And we can make good books affordable by selling used."

"I like the idea. Have you got a plan yet?"

"Just starting one. I'll bring them in, sort them in the back and lay out the shelves. But I have to develop sources. Maybe look at commercial dealers, or spend some time checking estate and yard sales."

"Excellent. I'll need a list of what you bring in and put out for sale to keep for inventory and add to the computer system. A spreadsheet would be nice. Price you paid plus list price. And the identifiers like title, author, edition. You know the drill."

"I do, and will get you a spreadsheet worked up once I start. You can tweak it as you need."

CHAPTER EIGHTEEN

"Bryan, what brings you all the way over here to my front door?"

"I had an extra few seconds and thought I would come over."

"New developments in the case?"

"Nothing new on yours. But I did hear something interesting about the Lester Owen's case."

"OK, the Lester news first. Then I need to tell you something about my case."

"The word written in blood on the antenna dish was despoiler."

"Despoiler? That's odd. Not exactly what I thought it was going to be."

"You mean it is somewhat sophisticated for these parts."

"Yeah. I was expecting something with four letters or some variation."

"Our populace is getting educated, what with a bookstore and all."

"You know what I mean. How many people around here use the word despoiler? I wouldn't even use it."

"It is a conundrum. We should pontificate upon the ramifications of the miscreant's deeds."

"Showoff. Hey, wasn't that the title of the television series about the zombie apocalypse filmed around Woodbury?"

"No, but it was the title of that terrible movie they shot here about an alien invasion. The Cove was supposed to be an ancient landing zone for UFOs. The enraged aliens came back with a vengeance. But apparently they did not bring a plot with them, because the movie did not have one."

"The antenna dishes were part of the SETI program at one time, weren't they?"

"What is SETI?"

"The Search for Extraterrestrial Intelligence or something like that. Some scientists were looking into space for evidence of aliens. Listening for radio waves and other signals coming from alien civilizations."

"I believe I heard that but can't attest to it."

"The dishes looking for alien life could be associated with the bad alien movie. Maybe Lester went out to the Cove to make a statement for publicity or something. Or maybe he was drunk. Then somebody killed him."

"Autopsy said very little alcohol was in his system, and no illegal drugs. And how many people his age would climb up in one of those things?"

"Unfortunate that the only person that knows isn't talking. But maybe while he was up there he saw an alien."

"That is about as reasonable as anything else I've heard. Now what do you have for me?"

"You can close the file on my shooting."

"It does not really work like that, where a victim requests case closures. Besides, why should I close it?"

"I found out who did it. A big misunderstanding. We had a talk and everything is good now."

"James, you might think it is over, but it isn't. There are still laws against discharging a firearm on campus. And likely a charge of reckless conduct."

"I know, but I'm satisfied with where things stand."

"Are you going to tell me who did it?"

"If I do, will you talk to the person and possibly make an arrest?"

"I might. That is generally how it works."

"What is the statute of limitations?"

"Should be two years for those charges. But since the suspect is unknown, the clock does not start until they are identified."

"I guess I'll have to get back to you. I'm just not sure when."

"You really aren't going to tell me?"

"Nope.

"OK, I can offer a compromise. You tell me who you think it was. They become a suspect and the clock starts. I might have to meet them to make it official. If there is no evidence, then there is not much I can do officially. Once the two-year clock is timed out they can tell me themselves, if they want to. The prosecutor knows he can't prosecute, and the case is closed."

"Can I discuss that with my legal advisor?"

"Sure. Can you afford another dollar?"

"Probably. I sold a book this month, so that gives me a two-dollar profit."

"I thought you authors lived the high life."

"I'm not that kind of author. You must be referring to the ultra successful best-selling ones."

"Yeah, those people."

"When you see the Maserati parked out front, you'll know I joined those ranks."

"Well, think about what I said and go see Larry."

"I will. Thanks for the information on Lester. Not that it helps much."

"Just find a handwriting expert that specializes in large letters written in blood."

"Sure, that will be easy."

I pedaled to town. Lottie was on shift at Mable's and I wanted her to look up Duffy in the official records. He might not even exist but perhaps there was some clue to his past if there was a record. I sat at the bar and waited for Lottie to cruise past on the way out of the kitchen.

"Lottie, do you know a man named Duffy who lives in the Cove?"

"A last name would help."

"I don't even know if he has one."

"Are you being dense again? Everybody around here has two names, most often three. Only people with one name are in California or overseas."

"Let me call someone. I'll get back to you in a minute."

"No, I'll get back to you when I refill your tea."

I called Sam's number. There was no answer, so I called Irene. I asked her if she knew Duffy's last name. She told me it was most likely Simmons. I thanked her and hung up. A few minutes later Lottie brought a pitcher of tea to give me a refill.

"Hey Lottie his last name is—"

"Simmons, Duffy Simmons."

"If you already knew why did you want me to find out?"

"Can't do everything for you. It was a lesson that you need to come prepared."

"Yes ma'am."

"What do you need?"

"Any information you can find on him. The usual official stuff."

"I'll take a quick look next break."

"Thanks."

I ordered the garden omelette again. Whatever was ripe in the garden was thrown into the eggs, along with cheese. It changed about every three days, and now it rarely even got listed on the board. A veggie Russian roulette, but it was almost always good. Except for the time beets were added. I hated beets anyway, but it turns out most people don't like eggs that look blood red.

After I finished Lottie came out and sat down on the stool beside me. "What the county has is nothing," she said. "No birth certificate on file, no social security records. That makes tracing or tracking him nearly impossible in an official way."

"What about unofficial?"

"According to sources from that side of the county, there

is no known father. His mother died some years ago. I found her information but there was little enough on her. She had a small place on a few acres in the Cove and mostly kept to herself. Duffy is reportedly her son. As I said, not officially, but everyone there knows that was her boy. He lives at her old place and from what I could find he never went to school. As I said, for all practical purposes he does not officially exist. If you want to know more, it might take a few days."

"Interesting, but we know he does exist. I'm wondering how he gets by. There must be something on record, like paying the electric bill or the mortgage, or even property taxes."

"You would think so, but even that is mostly missing. What is interesting is that the mother's property was paid off and rests in a trust. It pays the property taxes, but that is all."

"What do you know bout the trust?"

"Nothing other than it exists. It resides with an attorney's office in Woodbury."

"Somebody has to know something. There cannot be many trusts set up with a nearly non-existent beneficiary in the Cove."

"If anybody knows, they are not talking. At least officially. Or maybe it is an old trust. But doesn't matter, I can guarantee the lawyers won't talk to you."

"OK, have you heard any gossip or rumors?"

"The rumor from long ago is about Lester and his many girlfriends. More than one went away for a few months. Duffy's mother might have been one of them, but she stayed put instead."

"You are saying that old rumors put Lester as Duffy's father."

"There is that crack investigative mind working overtime."

"But is there any way to verify that since Duffy does not have any official paperwork or designation?"

"No, not without a DNA test."

"I guess it does not matter since Lester is dead anyhow. Unless Lester has anything that went into his estate that Duffy might inherit."

"Lester was broke. He was in debt and living on loans guaranteed by his house and vehicles."

"Then Duffy would not get anything, anyway."

"Other than Lester's personal possessions in the house, Duffy would get nothing. He might not even know Lester."

"I wonder if there are other trusts set up."

"None I know of. Duffy's mom might be the only one, since she must have refused to leave or give up the baby. I imagine the rest of the women did both."

"I doubt it matters. The trust is not a motivation for murder or much of anything except my curiosity."

"Curiosity does not pay the bills."

"Nor does it help you win the betting pool the Octoposse has either."

"No, it does not. Go get busy and tell me if you get a lead."

"I could not do that, it would give you inside help."

"That is the best kind. With this group there is no such thing as cheating. Because everyone does it."

Back home I called Larry. I trusted Bryan, but I did not know the prosecutor. If they were bored or ambitious, I worried they might try to push my shooting case instead of letting it sit.

"Lawrence Endicott, entrepreneur extraordinaire," was how he answered my call.

"I really hope that salutation was only meant for me. If that is your new slogan the kids at school are going to beat you up."

"I can't use my old slogan."

"What was it?"

"Better call Law-rence."

"Even worse. But I do have a legal question for you."

"Go for it. Me and my tennis ball will listen and advise."

"I had a talk with the person who shot at me. Everything is good. I told Bryan to close the case but he won't. Says the statute of limitations is only two years on the couple of misdemeanors that could be charged, but the clock only starts when a suspect is identified. He thinks he can call the person a suspect, then run out the clock so the prosecutor won't be able to press charges. Does any of that sound plausible?"

"Do you trust Bryan?"

"Yes, but I don't know about the prosecutor."

"Too many unanswered questions and possibilities. Best to have the person contact me directly, or you can bring them if they will agree to meet with me."

"They kind of already have."

"What?"

"Yeah, I think you two had dinner."

"James, I really need her to talk to me. There could be a way to make it go away but I'll need some details, and I'll need time to think about the kind of case the prosecutor might try. There could be a felony charge lurking."

"OK, I'll ask her to come to your office and you can tell us what might work."

"Good, and the sooner the better. Does anybody else know?"

"Just you, me and she."

"That is good news at least. Tell her to come over soon."

CHAPTER NINETEEN

Lee and Kim arrived in a pickup truck with a camper top. The truck was a typical university vehicle, showing too many miles and too little maintenance. Budgets barely paid for gas; anything else had to come from grant funds, and those were rapidly drying up. In my lifetime I expected to see the end of the grand university experiment in America.

But meanwhile, I greeted the graduate students in the parking lot near the garden. Lee was the mule and began unloading the truck. Kim began setting up a table and laying out computer components, along with a large battery system that probably weighed more than she did. I helped by pulling some large boxes out, while Lee tackled the GPR machine itself. It reminded me of a strange floor sander. Lee slowly rolled it down a makeshift ramp made from wood. He had plenty of practice with it so I stayed out of the way.

Once they had everything set up, we went to the area I had staked out with orange marker flags. I described what I was looking for and gave them an idea of where I thought the water main was located.

"Doctor Wilder, do you have an idea of how large the suitcase might be, and do you know on which side of the water main it might be?" Kim asked.

"I believe it would be about the same size as a large duffel bag today. Probably leather, and containing clothes. I'm not sure if there was anything metal in it. Possibly a belt buckle or watch." I was trying to describe what might be down there without telling them it was a body. I hoped their machine was not capable of showing human bones, especially a skull if it was still intact. "I know the water main runs parallel to the road, and I think it is about here. The suitcase should be on this side of the water pipe. It is probably about four or five feet deep. But my interpretation of the measurements written so long ago might be off. And please call me James, I no longer use my professional title."

"That is a good enough description for us to start," Lee said. "Kim, what should we try first, so you can set up and calibrate the system?"

"Start here and run perpendicular to the road, here between the cabbage and peas. Go about fifteen feet in a straight line. I want to get an idea of the soil consistency and then how the water main looks when you cross it."

I spent the next hour watching as Lee ran the machine across the soil, trying to miss most everything in the garden.

Luckily almost all the space I had tagged was either fallow or had a cover crop growing. Kim watched the screen and made notes, then directed Lee to rerun a line, or move to a different area. I was close enough to see the screen and saw nothing but squiggly lines of static. I saw Millard in his chariot rolling past us on the road. He waved and had a smile on, so I knew I'd be having a discussion with him later.

Basically Lee ran the GPR device back and forth across the rectangular area longways, then did it all over again going back and forth across the short side of the rectangle. Then Kim directed him to go back and check a few specific spots. Lee put down blue flags in one spot. Then another set in a line across my marked area. Finally, they were done.

"James, I think we have enough information to give you an initial analysis of the test area," Kim said.

"Do you have enough data to locate the suitcase? I'd really hate to bring in a backhoe to dig everything up."

"Possibly. The line of blue flags is where the water main should lie. The other blue flags indicate the area of an anomaly about four and a half feet down. It is the only disturbance I was able to find that could indicate a buried suitcase or similar object. Do you want us to help you dig that location?"

"Oh no, that is not necessary. I don't want to dig anything right now and disturb the garden. It can wait until the early spring when we plow that spot. If it has been there for eighty years, another few months won't hurt."

"True, it won't make any difference."

"I appreciate you and Lee coming over. I hear you are interested in the area around the springs. Would you like to see it since you are here?" I really wanted to move the conversation away from them helping me dig up a body.

"That would be great. I know the immediate area around the springs has been thoroughly disturbed when they put the pools in, and now it is a protected historical spot. But I wanted to check a hundred yard radius for potential dig sites that would not cause a problem."

"Sure, let's go."

The three of us walked around while Lee took pictures and Kim made notes on her phone. They found a couple of sites that looked promising away from the pools of Warm Springs themselves. One was across the road and on the edge of the golf course. My intent to get them to forget about my "suitcase" worked well, as they were both excited over what they saw near the springs. Now I just had to get back some night and dig up whatever was under the blue flags.

There was no reason to wait any longer. I had the spot tagged, and it needed to be excavated. I called the number on the maid service card Sabrina had given me. No answer so I left a message for her to meet me at my house.

I also called Vicky. I told her about the conversation with Bryan, and that I had discussed it with Larry. He had reservations that he needed to think about. She asked me what I thought, and my response was to get with Larry. He would give her good advice. Possibly even talk to another lawyer, since they would also keep the conversation confidential. If she took that course, I would be happy to go with her or give her a note to take. I thought that the "victim," me, knowing what Vicky had done and not pressing charges could bolster her case. The other course of action was doing nothing and not telling anyone, as we had been doing. She said she would visit Larry first and then let me know.

Sabrina called an hour later. She seemed quieter than usual.

"Sabrina, I need a favor. But it is a little outside your job description."

"If it is not too crazy, I'm probably authorized to assist. What is it?"

"Are you good with a shovel?"

"OK, I guess. Why?"

"I need to dig up and move a body."

"Oh, so the stories about you are true."

"It is not what you think. The body was buried before I was born, but it is in a bad place and needs to be moved."

"I will help, but I have a condition."

"OK, what is it?"

"You have to tell me all about the body and how it got there. Then how you know about it. That must be a good story, and after watching you for day after tedious day I need some relief."

"I can do that. Come over for a late snack tonight to talk about it. Then we will go move the body. Although I don't expect much to be left after eighty years."

Sabrina came to the house at 11 pm. Kat was happy to see her again.

"Would you like some hot tea or coffee?" I asked. "Maybe iced tea?"

"Coffee is good. What are these oat bars?"

"British flapjacks. But made to US standards as they mimic s'mores with chocolate and marshmallow bits."

"You are bribing me with what you would feed a kid? But they are tasty whatever they are."

"Glad you like them. I have a box made so you can take some with you."

"That is awfully mom-ish of you."

"Got to keep you happy and alert. While you are here, there might also be a spider in the bathroom that needs killing."

"If it is poisonous, I'll just plop it under your pillow."

"That is not very guardian-angelish of you. Let's walk."

"Where are we going?"

"Just down the hill to the golf course, where the campus garden is located."

"That is a dumb place to bury a body."

"It was 80 years ago so I think things were a little different around here."

"You are definitely going to tell me the story."

"It is a long one."

"We have at least two hours of digging if it is four of five feet deep. We have plenty of time."

"I guess we do. OK, a long time ago in a galaxy far away, lived some people on the Roosevelt campus in Warm Springs."

"Stop there. Just tell me the story, don't put me to sleep. Otherwise you will be digging by yourself."

"OK, I'll tell you when we get there."

We walked down to the garden. I had left two shovels at the garden earlier in the day as I didn't want anyone seeing me carrying shovels at night. That tends to make people suspicious. At the site, I handed Sabrina a pair of work gloves. No reason to risk blisters.

"How do you manage to stay in the woods during the day while watching me?" I asked.

"It is not easy. I listen to music, use lots of bug spray, and sweat a lot."

"And you have time to think."

"That is an overrated pursuit these days."

We began to dig where the cluster of blue flags indicated a soil disturbance a few feet down. I began the story of finding the bottle, getting the letter inside deciphered, and what it meant, or at least my interpretation of it. Sabrina did not interrupt as we dug. We took a break after 45 minutes.

"You must think the letter is valid since we are now digging for a body," she said.

"I found a newspaper article about a young man being hit by a train that coincided with dates mentioned in the letter. But not much on the other missing young man. I did locate his family in New York. Digging this site is the best way to verify the story. Besides, if there is anything at all left, I want the remains out from under the garden."

"It is just fertilizer at this point. And nothing you are growing has roots deep enough to get down that far if that is what you are worried about."

"Still, I will know it is there. If anyone ever found out I'm also concerned it might get the garden shut down."

"I get it. In about another 45 minutes you will have your answer if there is anything left. Is that what the metal mesh wire is for?"

"Yes, once we get to the right depth, there might be some soil discoloration. We will shovel that dirt onto the wire mesh. Shake it a little to sift the dirt away from any remains larger than one-fourth inch."

"A real archaeological dig."

Sabrina's estimate of the time left was too optimistic. As the hole deepened it got harder to throw the dirt upward, and the hole was small enough we got in each others way. That was solved by taking turns in the hole; one dug for five minutes while the other rested, then we switched.

An hour later, the flashlight showed dirt that was a little darker than the loose clay mixed with sand we had been digging through.

"OK, now we throw this discolored layer onto the wire mesh," I said.

"Two shovel-fulls deep across the discolored area should be enough," Sabrina replied.

"I think so, unless we see something else."

About four shovels of dirt filled the wire. I pulled it around the garden for several feet which helped the loose dirt fall through and leave the rocks and dirt clods. There was nothing that looked like bones. Then on the third round of wire pulling, when I used the flashlight I saw something white.

"Sabrina, we might have something." She got out of the hole and we used our gloves to move the dirt around and sift through the wire. Our reward was three teeth. White but stained from the red clay.

"I think that proves your letter was correct."

"I think so too. No dental records that far back to be able to prove who the owner was, but this seems to show there was a human body here."

We spent another half hour digging and sifting. The effort netted twelve teeth and what I first thought was a piece of broken pottery. When I picked it up, I could tell the weight and texture was wrong, and it was more likely a piece of skull. We dug a little more and sifted but the only other thing was a small chunk of corroded metal that might have been a pocket watch. The Georgia soil had done its job and disposed of a whole human after eighty years.

"OK, Sabrina, let's fill this hole back in and get out of here."

Thirty minutes later we were walking back to the house. Gravity was on our side filling in the hole so it went a lot faster. I had the teeth and piece of skull in a bag. The metal was in my pocket. I still was not sure what to do with all of it so I'd keep it for now. At least I would not worry anymore about what was under the garden. But the bag in my hand was beginning to weigh on me.

Back at my house Sabrina drank some tea before she left to do whatever she did. I told Sabrina I had found the shooter and cleared up the misunderstanding.

"A rifle shot is not a misunderstanding," she said. "It is a clear statement."

"I agree, but the underlying cause was an emotional response to a traumatic event. I got blamed, and shot at as a warning, but now it is cleared up. I'll be calling Atlanta tomorrow so maybe you can finally go home." She didn't look happy nor give the response of joy I had expected.

"Sure. Maybe I'll see you before I go."

"Sabrina, do you really want to go back?"

"What I want to do and what I have to do, don't always match up."

"Maybe I'll wait a few more days to make the call. After all, I did wait until I could enlist you in a grave robbery."

"Don't think I didn't notice."

"Come over for a meal tomorrow. We can have some decent food and talk more."

"Maybe. I'll let you know by text. Right now I'm going home to take a shower and sleep."

"Thanks for helping tonight."

"You are welcome. It's another crime I can put on my resume."

"Don't forget your box of flapjacks."

CHAPTER TWENTY

"Just coffee and a pastry," I said. "That new crème brûlée donut might have my name on it."

"The same name as on the room in ICU at the hospital after your cardiac event?" Lottie asked.

"Just coffee."

"Wise choice."

"Lottie, can you check on a Charles Robinson? He owns the billboard place in Woodbury. I'm curious if he has or had family in Hamilton County."

"Give me some hours and I'll let you know. After Lester and Duffy, you know this is the third favor you've asked for the last few days. Time to up the charges."

"I would ask someone else, but you are the best source in the county."

"Flattery won't work on me."

"What about flowers?"

She stopped for a second in thought. "Flowers would be nice." It was probably the most un-Lottie-like thing I'd ever heard.

"Then flowers it is. Thanks."

I came back with flowers. Late season sunflowers and some other nice blooms were at the florist in Manchester. I didn't know what Lottie liked, but thought the blend would have some she preferred. She actually smiled when I brought them in and set them on the counter. I would start bringing flowers to both Mable's and the bookstore.

"I got some stuff on the feller you asked about," Lottie said.

"Thanks for looking."

"He has been in the county about ten years. Early on he was in Savannah and that is where he got into billboards. Then he moved to Atlanta and worked for some big companies. He opened his own company in Macon and did well enough that a major company bought him out. That is when he came here and started another, smaller company."

"Even though this is a small market he must be doing well."

"Good enough to pay his employees well and apparently still turn a profit. Not like he has any competition for twenty-five miles in any direction."

"Any idea where he is originally from?"

"That was easy. Birth certificate was filed here in Hamilton County. No other records of him here so he must have moved away when he was young."

"Any interesting gossip or rumors about him?"

"Nothing that I have heard. Not surprising that his early years were quiet."

"Why is that?"

"Address from the birth certificate shows his family was in the Cove at the time. Folks there tend to be clannish. But if you knew somebody there, I bet you could find out more."

"What about since he's been back?"

"Not much. Does not seem to have any enemies, personal or political. Blends into the community and is about as exciting as a slice of sandwich bread. Seems to be civic-minded and contributes to good causes."

"I guess a lot worse things could be said about somebody."

"Sure could. You, for example. Nothing but trouble on two legs since you got here."

"I'm just trying to make your life more interesting."

"Getting shot in the head was an excessive gesture to give me two sentences of gossip."

"Technically I was not shot in the head. And besides, it was a misunderstanding."

"See, somebody misunderstands you and tries to blow your brains out. Most people would just get a rude hand gesture."

"You might have a point."

"Of course I do. Now get out to the Cove and find out more about Charles. But remember, most people out there are better shots. Lots of stories about buried bodies around. Mostly strangers asking questions."

Charles was a solid contender on the list of murder suspects, based on his past and access to tall ladders. I definitely needed to go the Cove and ask around about him, at least with the one native I knew there. I was not intimidated by Lottie's comments. I'd grown up hearing the same talk about the mountain hollers hosting my maternal ancestors. The only people that went missing were those that really wronged somebody's family or federal revenue agents. Surely the Cove was just as reasonable.

Before that I was going to talk to Charles myself. I had a somewhat believable story that might get me into a conversation with him. I went to his Woodbury office first, but the lone receptionist told me he was out at the yard. The overall office was small, with perhaps three offices. The back of the open room contained a computer and several printers, including one large poster printer. An oversized conference table was likely where they laid out the billboard designs. I thanked the receptionist and left. She was calling ahead to let him know I'd arrive in a few minutes.

The billboard yard on the road outside Woodbury was a large lot surrounded by a chain-link fence. Everything within sight was clean and tidy. Two metal warehouse buildings and a large concrete pad covered with a metal roof. Two trucks were parked under it, while two other large trucks were in front of one warehouse. A half dozen cars and trucks were parked in a row in front of the other building. I parked along those vehicles. By the time I got out and made it to the building, a large blonde man younger than me approached. He was wearing a Robinson Billboard polo shirt so he must be official.

"Janice called and told me somebody was looking for me. You must be him."

"I must be. I'm James Wilder from Warm Springs. You must be Charles."

"I must be. I even have the shirt to prove it. What can I do for you?"

"I was hoping you might have five minutes to talk about billboards."

"That conversation would be more like five hours. And if you are buying one, it will be longer than that."

"Oh, my interests are more of a practical or technical nature. I'm a writer, and I have a character that does something stupid and gets stranded on a high billboard. I wanted to ask a few questions before I wrote about something I knew nothing about."

"I see. Normally wouldn't you just make something up?"

"I do it all the time. But I am guessing in your business there are safeguards to prevent someone from getting up on a billboard. That said, it seems those same safeguards would probably get a person back down safely. I'm looking for the mechanism to get him up but then get him stranded."

"OK, I understand."

"I see billboards all the time but rarely pay any attention to details. So how can you get on one? A ten-foot ladder, but then that gets knocked over somehow?"

"You really don't know how billboard access works then. Let's walk around the yard and I'll do a little show and tell."

"That would be great."

"You don't need anything regarding the advertising side of the business I take it?"

"Probably not. But, if the character went up on the billboard to try to tear it down because he didn't like what it said it could come into play. Do you get complaints about content or people trying to deface your boards?"

"We always have a few complaints. The board is in the

wrong spot, or it is too big or too bright. The content is wrong or offensive. Then others complaining about it being too small, either the board or the text, or it is not lit up enough."

"Can't please everyone?"

"Sometimes it is like you can't please anyone. But now I'm complaining. Let's get you a brief tour and answer your questions."

"Sounds good." We walked past the two large trucks outside. A large metal pipe lay on the ground.

"This is the base pole for most of our typical installations. You have to imagine it is standing up after being set on a base of concrete. At the top would be a catwalk and the board structure. There you see the welded-on ladder in the middle section of the pipe."

"If it was standing up, there is about a ten or twelve foot section at the bottom without a ladder, then ten feet of ladder, then just pipe again for ten or twelve feet."

"That's right. Can you guess why?"

"The missing ladder on the bottom keeps people from climbing unless they bring their own ladder to access the welded ladder. But once they get to the top of it, there is still a big gap with no access to get on up to the catwalk."

"Exactly. And almost nobody has a special ladder they carry up more than twenty feet of other ladders and then fasten it to get up the last section of pipe."

"Then why have the welded ladder at all?"

"Because we have the ladders to attach to the top and bottom to let our guys get up and down for minor jobs if they don't need to carry much. Also it is a safety factor as it is really a backup ladder."

"There must be a way for them to get up easier than climbing those ladders."

"Yep. Let's walk over to those trucks." One was black and the other white. There was not a Robinson Billboard logo on either one. "See what is in the oversized bed? It is a special system that provides a stable and angled ladder up to 40 feet for our guys to access most boards. For other boards we also have a lift bucket truck like you see the power companies use."

I was looking at several sections of a wide metal ladder that I imagined would telescope up to the billboard. "These are more like a wider version of a ladder truck the fireman use."

"Yep, same concept but specialized for our business. Not everybody has them but I feel these are the safest option for most of our boards. The ladder is four feet wide for better stability."

"I guess safety is an issue for work up that high."

"It is, and the cost of my liability policy reflects it. Some guys can do this kind of work and some can't."

"You must have harnesses and safety lines and all kinds of things like that."

"I do, because I insist on everyone using them plus other measures. I won't tolerate anyone not being safe. Take a look in the cab." He opened the door of the black truck. Inside it was a typical truck cab, but I saw some modifications. "See that camera on the dash? They are required to keep it on while driving in case of any accidents. It is also adjustable so when they get to the job site, the camera stays on the billboard, to show the ground up to the catwalk. If there is an accident, and luckily there has not been, we would know what caused it.

"My guys also carry a safety button on their vests. They press it and we get an emergency call. That case on the seat is a satellite phone. That keeps my people connected no matter where they are.

"This cabinet is something special and I require it in all the trucks I own. It is a first aid kit worthy of the military. Plus it has sunscreen, bug spray, and those epinephrine injectors."

"I get the bug spray and sunscreen since they are out in the weather a lot," I said. "But why the injectors?"

"One of our top worker injury categories are stings. Bees, wasps, hornets, and every other ornery stinging creature can be found on a billboard."

"That makes sense. You must screen your board workers for sting allergies."

"We do, but I also know that somebody that has been stung for thirty years with no reaction can suddenly develop an anaphylactic reaction to bee venom."

"You seem to have all your bases covered."

"I try to. Some things I can't control, like the weather. But my people are required to keep a weather alert radio on when on a board. That is also in every truck. We have been lucky and had no close calls with lightning."

"I never knew how dangerous this work is."

"Most people don't. Now you see why we do what we can to keep people off the boards. If it is dangerous to my trained workforce, it is more so for the typical teenager wanting to impress his girlfriend or spray some graffiti. Is that what your character was planning?"

"Something like that. I originally wanted him to climb a water tower, but that has been done many times in books."

"Those are even more dangerous than boards. But there are still a lot of old ones that can be climbed."

"I do appreciate your time today. I've learned a lot and will change my book because of it."

"That is a good idea. Come by again if you need something else. Especially if you need a board to advertise your book."

"Probably not a bad idea. But I don't think that is in my part-time author budget."

Driving home and thinking, I knew there were two important things I had learned about Charles Robinson. He was very safety conscious, and he definitely had the ability to get Lester's body on the antenna dish.

Before following that lead further, I needed to change gears again. The last weeks I felt I had been all over the place, chasing my shooter, looking into Lester's death, and fighting off Benjamin. Plus getting introduced to Sabrina and thinking about my murders from the guest cottage letter. I turned toward Hamilton to get another plan into action.

Vicky was sitting in front of Larry's desk. Larry was still bouncing his tennis ball with one hand and writing notes with the other. I got no indication that anything was going on, but having those two in the same room made me nervous, anyway.

"Oh, sorry Larry, I didn't know you had a client."

"James, so good to see you." Vicky bounced off the chair and gave me a quick hug. "Larry is helping with a life plan to get everything in order."

"And we are planning how to respond to Bryan's plan," Larry said. "James, what can I help you with?"

"Without going into details, you know that folder I recently reviewed?"

"Yes, what would you like me to do?"

"If you have not already, I think it is time to release the kraken."

"Ah, OK. Vicky and I were just talking about the same subject. But since she is a separate client, she will have to give me permission to speak about the shared matter?"

"Are you talking about Pamela Foster?" Vicky asked. "Yes, let's get the plan in action. I want that woman out of my life."

"I think it best for everyone in Warm Springs," I said.

"Consider it done," Larry said. "Vicky, when I finish this we will go over what we need to do and get Pamela Foster dealt with."

CHAPTER TWENTY-ONE

After my previous conversation with Dunder, I was convinced he had not killed Lester. He could have and then lied to me, but my instinct was he had not. Charles was more interesting. He had the means to place the body, but so far I did not have a motive for him. But there was a Cove connection of some sort.

My initial list also had the sporting goods store owner as a potential suspect. Mainly because they had more types and shapes of ladders than anyone in the county. That was due to having the most tree stands used by deer hunters in the region. They might have a special ladder or hoist capable of moving a body up thirty feet above the ground. I doubted it was a viable trail but I might as well stop by.

Half the parking lot was full of elaborate ground-based and elevated deer hunting stands. Hunter comfort had come a long way since I used to freeze ten feet up in a tree sitting on a board. Some of these were probably wired for cable so as not to miss the Saturday game. All that was needed was a plush recliner and a cell phone antenna for a portable man cave. The deer must be a lot safer with all the distracted hunters around. If the guest cottage never got finished, I could buy one of these as a guest house. What I did not see were any sturdy 30-foot tall ladders.

I went in to see the usual hunting store patrons wearing camouflage gear and talking with the men behind the counter. I looked at a few of the old-style tree stands inside the store. Even a few climbing stands like those I remembered from the bad old days.

"Can I help you?" asked a store employee.

"I'm looking for a new stand."

"Do you like these? Not very comfortable but easy to carry and move around."

"I've already spent too much of my life miserable in one of these."

"We have some nice ones outside."

"I saw those and they are nice."

"Want to go take a tour?"

"Possibly. But what I'm looking for may not be possible."

"We can make most anything work."

"I'm looking for a stand about thirty feet high."

"Thirty feet? That is above our usual installation limit. We might could do it, but it would be expensive and even then would void the warranty. Our liability insurance might not even cover that. Does it have to be that high?"

"For this particular field it does."

"If you get one that high you'll need to spend some time

target practicing out of it. That is a steep shooting angle for anything close. Even long shots will need a slight elevation change on the scope."

"I know it will be an adjustment. Do you have anything in stock that tall?"

"I don't. I'd have to check the computer to see if anything is available. I can tell you none of the ones outside can go that high without a lot of extra support under them."

"Have you ever put up anything that high around here?"

"No, but I did a special one at 25 feet last year. A deluxe model that weighed a thousand pounds. We rented a small crane for setup. It was expensive to build up the support and platform. But the customer did not care about cost."

"I may have to rethink the height. If I moved it, I could take ten feet off the height."

"That is much better, but still more costly than our standard stands."

"I'll go back out to my place and look at other sites. Maybe find something closer to a standard height. I appreciate your time."

"Let us know if we can help you."

"Thanks again."

I could take the sporting goods place, including the owner, workers, and their customers off the suspect list. The crane rental was an idea I could check on, but those were obvious and slow to move around. They would likely have been seen in the Cove, even at night, in front of the dish closest to the road.

Later that evening I flashed my lights three times. I wanted to test out the semi-facetious signal plan I had mentioned to Sabrina. I had snacks and decided to share them, if she was even in the area. But a few minutes later she appeared on the back porch.

"I thought you might have left for the night," I said.

"Thought about it. The gnats have been bad today."

"This is silly. The threat is over. Why don't you just take the other bedroom, or the guest cottage if you want to rough it? You will still be on assignment but a lot more comfortable."

"I'll think about it."

"While you are here I'll fix some food. Now, what do you normally do, at least before you got the posh assignment of hanging out in the woods?"

"I'm mostly on the computer. Fifty percent of the business is now about information and how to use it against people to make money."

"Sounds like the tech bros of Silicon Valley."

"Similar business model. But we are more local and have better job perks."

"Sabrina, you said something the other night about the old stories about me. What were you referring to?"

"I heard you had unique ways of dealing with difficult clientele. The implication was you had innovative ways of hurting people."

"Those stories are not true, in the sense that I didn't physically hurt anybody. None of that is needed if you know a little about psychology, and let people's imaginations do all the work."

"What does that mean?"

"My young colleagues at the time thought every problem was a baseball."

"Because they had baseball bats?"

"Exactly. And if that didn't work, other weapons. I found all that unnecessary."

"I don't know how you were effective without those threats."

"I considered having to resort to violence as a failure. It was an inefficient use of effort. None of it made sense to me."

"Why did you leave? It seems you had a system worked out.

"Although I dispensed with the physical violence, scaring people is still violence. Even though the few people I dealt with were criminals of various sorts, it still bothered me."

"You must have had a good system to scare them so effectively."

"It was pretty simple. Just had to think ahead and study the classics."

"I don't get it. But I think you are enjoying drawing out the story."

"I'll get to the point. Use a creepy, scary place like an abandoned warehouse with a bolted-down chair on a concrete floor. Pour out some ketchup or tomato paste and let it dry. Have a toolbox with all kinds of sharp or weird tools and some medical instruments. Bring in the mark and let them sit and think about what they see.

"That usually did it. But if not I'd come in wearing some old hospital scrubs with dried tomato sauce and do my rendition of an inquisitor. For threats I would recall details from a few specific history books. Humans have been torturing humans for thousands of years and writing about it. I picked out some ugly scenarios that I could remember.

"Give them more time to digest all they saw, and what it portended, as I pulled items out of the toolbox like a bad movie. And that was my brief foray in the Atlanta mob scene. Less than a year if I remember."

"I don't think you are telling me everything. I heard about other things you did."

"Anything else was just me being a stupid teenager, and not even for the business. Getting into minor trouble with other boys my age was common back then."

"Sure it was."

"That was mostly true. Sabrina, I don't know your situation or much of anything about you. Therefore, I'm trying to not be presumptuous. If you have no interest in what I'm about to say I won't take it personally."

"Just say it already. Otherwise you are putting me to sleep."

"Fine. As I have mentioned before, you don't have to stay in the business if you don't want to."

"Is that it?"

"Yep."

"Are you implying I'm like you and want out?"

"Not at all, because I don't know you. But the old guys in Atlanta told me something that I still remember."

"What was it?"

"They told me to get out if I wanted to. But do it sooner rather than later. By the time you hit thirty you will be in forever. The money is too good to give up, and by then you have done enough unsavory things that you won't feel good about even if you did get out."

"That makes some sense, I guess."

I noticed a car coming into campus via the side road by my house. When there were only three cars an evening on the road, any car gets noticed. This one was familiar. It turned toward the house then into the driveway. Sabrina tensed and was about to slip off the porch.

"This is a friend. No reason to leave."

"Are you sure?"

"Yes, and I doubt it will take long."

I walked through the house and opened the front door. "Hi Donna, I wasn't expecting you."

"Hi James. I know, but I was going past campus and thought I'd stop in for a few moments. Is that OK?"

"Sure, come on back. We're sitting on the porch."

Donna followed me and then stopped when she saw Sabrina. "James, I didn't know you had company."

"Donna, this is Sabrina." Donna, an attractive woman in a dress, and Sabrina, an attractive younger woman in black motorcycle leathers, stood looking at each other. I sensed an unnatural tension.

"Hello," Donna said. "James, I need to go. This was a bad idea."

"It is OK, Donna. Sabrina and I were just talking about old times."

"No, I have to go." Donna turned quickly to go back through the house. Sabrina had not said anything but had a strange look. I stood for a second trying to figure out what had just happened.

"James, is that your girlfriend?" Sabrina asked.

"We used to date. Now we are trying out the friends thing. But she seems upset."

"You idiot. Go talk to her, right now, before she leaves. She has the wrong idea about me being here."

"Oh, I see." I quickly went after Donna. She was already in her car and about to start it.

"Donna, please wait for a minute. I need to explain."

"James, you don't need to."

"Yes, I do. Sabrina is my, well, bodyguard."

"James, that is the dumbest thing you have ever told me. It makes me think that you think I am stupid."

"Uh, OK, let me try again. Sabrina is family. My Atlanta family."

Donna paused, processing what I had just said. She knew my history enough to know what I was implying, if she thought about it.

"Wait, you mean she is the Atlanta family you don't talk about?"

"Yes, that one. Sabrina is either a great niece or a third cousin. It is hard for me to keep them straight since I'm not around that side of the family. She was sent to keep an eye on me since the shooting."

"OK, I understand now."

"You can come back in if you want to."

"No, I shouldn't. But I would like to talk sometime."

"Me too. Can I call you later this week?"

"Yes, then we can meet for lunch."

"Good, I'll talk to you later."

As she drove off, I went back in and thought about what had just happened. It seemed obvious Donna had the wrong idea, but I had been slow to understand and react. I probably still would have been standing on the back porch if Sabrina had not told me to go after Donna. But I felt like I was still missing something.

"James, did you explain to her?" Sabrina asked.

"I did. She understands."

"You said she is your former girlfriend?"

"Yes."

"Let me guess. She ended it, because of some difference you two had, but she wanted to stay friends."

"Yes, that's right. How did you know?"

"By her reaction. You realize it is not really over, right?"

"What do you mean?"

"You will figure it out. I can't tell you everything. I need to go."

After Sabrina left, I mentally replayed the conversation with her after Donna left. I knew what she was implying. But Donna had ended our dating relationship, and it was really over. Now we were friends. She might have felt uncomfortable or even jealous when she saw Sabrina, but that did not mean much, in my mind. I had other issues to worry about, anyway.

CHAPTER TWENTY-TWO

"Duffy, one night when you were at the big dish, you said you saw a big black truck, or locomotive." I was back in the Cove and talking to Duffy on the side of the road. I needed to confirm details the night of Lester's murder.

"Yes, yes I did."

"Was there also a smaller, older truck there on the same night?"

"I don't want to say."

"Did the big black one bring the little blue one, or did somebody drive it?"

"It was a train, but just two engines and one conductor. Big black and little blue locomotor."

"The black one towed the blue one?"

"Just like a train."

"The black one left later. The blue one stayed at the dish, didn't it?"

"I don't want to say."

"It was a nice one, the blue one."

"It was small and smelled good, shiny and old. It just felt right."

"You know how to drive, don't you?"

"I don't want to say." He seemed nervous.

"It is OK to tell me. Did you know that Sam and Irene are my relatives? Not just my friends. That is why I come to the Cove. I visit them."

"It was something I learned to do when I was a boy. First locomotor was a big green one with three wheels."

"That sounds like a tractor."

"I've heard it called that. It was slow. But I learned about turning the wheel to make it go here or there, and moving the stick while pressing the pedals to go faster or slower. But I don't drive no more. These new locomotors, they don't feel right. They also don't smell right. Cannot abide them. No, they won't do at all."

"I understand. They are different. But an old, nice truck is easy. Smells and feels right. My grandfather had a truck just like the blue one. I used to ride with him to the Farmer's Market in Macon. He would sell pink-eye purple-hull peas. By the peck or the bushel."

"That is a really good bean. You can eat them raw before they get too big. Shell them out and drop them right into your mouth."

"I've done that. You probably liked the blue truck."

"It was nice. But it was left there and nobody was taking

care of it. It needed a home and I could not keep it. I don't have the drink it needs to keep going."

"Sam and Irene are nice people."

"They are. They let me pick in their garden. Then they go away and come back with the tiny sweetest blueberries. Those are good."

"I know, they let me have some, too. Duffy, did you find the blue truck a good home?"

"I did. It needed one. Nice people could need it. Was it a good thing?"

"It was."

"I never seen them drive it. I thought they are mad at me."

"Not at all. They are not mad. It is a nice truck, but they did not know where it came from. That is why you have not seen them drive it."

"I hoped they would like it."

"They do. Now that they know where it came from they can do something with it."

"You think so?"

"I do. They already have trucks, so they might have too many. Maybe you can talk to them and figure out if they should keep it or find another home for it in the Cove."

"Who else?"

"What about you? Do you want a nice blue truck?"

"I can't keep it. The drink it needs I don't have."

"That is true. But Sam and Irene can help you find it a home. Or find a tank with the drink fuel. I know Dunder has big tanks. Then it can be kept wherever, or with whoever." Duffy smiled but didn't say anything else. "Duffy, everything is good. You did good. I'll tell Sam and Irene if you want me to."

"Yes, yes please."

"Good. Then we can figure out where the blue truck can stay."

"I like that."

"Duffy, do you remember what the black truck did that night?"

"It acted strange. The railroad track went up with a man and a big bundle. He had a bucket. Then it came down and left."

"Thanks for telling me Duffy."

My next destination was just down the road. Then up the side of the crater to the blue house.

"Hi Irene. Is Sam around?"

"He is somewhere down the hill. I can call him and then you can meet him."

"Actually I'd like to talk to you both. I found out who brought you the nice blue truck."

"I'll call him. I'm sure he will be right up. Would you like some tea?"

"That would be nice."

We waited a few minutes before Sam came driving up. He got some tea, and we sat at the table.

"So, who was it that dumped the truck?" Sam asked.

"Duffy was out in the back dish the night the truck was brought out to the front dish," I said.

"Brought out? The sheriff thinks Lester went out there to meet someone that killed him. Then some kids stole the truck."

"The first part of that is false. You already know the second part is."

"Then what happened?"

"Duffy saw a large black truck tow Lester's truck out to the dish. The truck ran a large ladder up to the front dish. You know the rest. The blue truck stayed so it would look like Lester had driven there on his own. Duffy decided to give it a nice home. He left it in your driveway as a gift because you two have been nice to him."

"James, all this is a relief," Irene said. "But now the old questions come back up. Duffy can clear up a lot, and talk to the sheriff… Oh, maybe that is not a good idea."

"Right. Duffy probably should not be a witness for his own good. If he was, he would also tell where the truck went. You could probably talk your way out of it. Or get charged with evidence tampering."

"What should we do?"

"Keep the truck out of sight a while longer. I do not know how this is going to go. But I don't think it is finished yet."

"James, how much more involved are you going to get?"

"I'll dig around a little more but quietly. I need to satisfy my own curiosity. But I understand what you are saying about Lester. He did so much damage that people might not want to know the truth. Only that he is no longer around."

Back home I got the biggest surprise yet from Lester's death. Bryan was walking in front of the station beside my house and on his phone. He waved me down. I parked and waited for him to finish his call.

Bryan was far enough away that I could not hear anything specific. I heard him ask a few brief questions. Then he hung up and walked over to me.

"That was John Dixon on the phone. You can call off your hunt."

"What is going on?"

"John went back over the case with the coroner. Time of death, cause of death, body temperature. All that and more was reviewed again. There is no doubt that Lester died of a heart attack. The official report will state that Lester was alive when he climbed up in the dish to write something, and then died while doing it. No foul play."

"Huh, I was not expecting that."

"But there is something else that won't be announced. Although the heart attack can't be disputed, there is some forensic evidence, mainly body temperature, that Lester might have died elsewhere earlier, and was placed on the dish. John thinks he might find who did it by letting them think they are off the hook. He does that by reporting Lester died up on the dish."

"I guess that makes sense. The only missing piece of the puzzle is Lester's truck."

"John thinks Lester drove it out to the dish, and it was stolen from there. Probably will show up down at the river after some kids finish their joy ride. What do you think?"

"It could have happened that way, from the outside looking in. Gets rid of a lot of what-ifs and ties it up in a neat package. Maybe too neat."

"Uh oh, I sense the quest is on again."

"I'm not sure. I need some time to think about it. But my gut is giving me signals that not all is as it seems."

"It never is. We never know everything, you know that. Later we find out more, but even then some pieces never get put in the puzzle."

"Are you trying to talk me out of looking any further?"

"I'm using reverse psychology to keep you looking. I feel

the same way as you do. And once again, I'm glad John has this case and not me."

"Bryan, what is John Dixon's next move with the case?"

"The official report comes out tomorrow. He has pulled everyone off except one deputy. Instead of a murder case it is now just potential corpse desecration."

"Still a felony in Georgia isn't it?"

"Yes, but John still has a full county and its criminals to deal with. I'm sure he'd like to find and arrest the person who did it, but now it is a lower priority."

"I understand all that. But it was a bold move and kind of insulting to both Lester and the police to put him up on the dish."

"It was, and eventually somebody might talk. But I detect a hint of disappointment that it was not a murder."

"Not exactly disappointment. Maybe even more of an interest into what happened after the death and the motivation behind it."

"Yep, you are still on the case."

"Maybe. I think it was a personal vendetta. Enough hate there to move and place the body where it was displayed publicly. Oh, what about the blood? Was Lester bled out after the heart attack? I know it's hard to bleed an animal after it has been dead a while."

"The blood was not human. Came back from the state laboratory as deer blood."

"That won't narrow it down much."

"Archery season is already underway so the processors have deer blood. And every road has a dead deer on it at least once a week."

"So no murder, only possible corpse desecration for

moving and displaying the body. I see John's point of lowering the priority."

I left Bryan and stepped onto my place, where I needed to sit on the back porch and think a bit. I had kept a lot of information from Bryan. I did not feel too bad since he was not the investigator. I needed to reconsider everything anyway, before telling him, since it was no longer a murder.

I now realized I did not have to solve Lester's murder. My motivation in the case was to help Sam and Irene figure out who tried to frame them. But now that was no longer the issue. Although the truck, as evidence, was still a problem. I still wondered about who placed Lester's body, and why, but that was no longer worth a great deal of my time. The only thing left to deal with was how to help Sam get rid of an old truck. Everything was working out. All but the nagging feeling that Lester's death still did not make sense.

CHAPTER TWENTY-THREE

I was not giving up on the case, regardless of the sheriff's belief it was not a murder. Perhaps because I knew more about parts that the sheriff did not, but mainly because my gut told me something was off. Time to work leads on my prime suspect. Back to the Cove.

"Dunder, did you know a Robinson family that lived in the Cove? I don't think they were here very long, maybe a few years. It would have been some time ago."

"Maybe. The name might be familiar. Let me think on it."

"Take your time. There was a mom, dad, and a little boy during the time they lived in the Cove. I'm not sure of his age and whether you night have known him. Name was Charles Robinson."

"Charles Robinson? I remember a boy out here that was called Chuck. I do think he was a Robinson. Same person?"

"Probably. "

"Chuck's parents lost their jobs or got divorced or something. I don't remember the details."

"Was that why they left?"

"No, that wasn't it. Now I remember. They bought a house that Lester owned. A place Lester had gotten cheap, then he fixed it up a little. He sold it to them, but had fixed the contract so he could throw the tenants out at any time. He might have forged a page after it was signed. I would not put it past him. It was his major mistake."

"That sounds bad. But how was it a mistake?"

"Before then he had the cover of the Savings and Loan. He always blamed their policies for how he screwed people over. When he threw out Chuck's parents, everyone knew it was just Lester doing it. Everybody in the county realized what a snake he was. Nobody would buy anything from him after that. The S&L also started losing business. People in the Cove and most of Hamilton County could not trust a place run by Lester. But that was not the worst of it."

"What do you mean?"

"I heard later that Lester had suggested something heinous to the family. Nobody ever told me what it was. But it was bad enough that I remembered it when we went into business with him. That is why I never trusted him with all my money."

"Was the suggestion he made something that might get him killed?"

"Sounded like it. But it did not happen, obviously. That was a long time ago."

"Thanks, Dunder."

Driving back to Warm Springs I became more convinced

Charles might be the prime suspect. If nothing else, he probably put Lester's dead body up on the dish. He was also the only person in the county that I knew had a ladder truck.

He was a young boy when Lester threw his family out. But whatever Lester did would have made an impact on Charles, at least through the parents and their suffering.

On the way home I got a call from Larry. We normally did not talk on the phone so I answered instead of letting it go to voice mail.

"Pamela Foster is no longer a problem. At Vicky's house she brought up her close relationship with a state senator. Plus a lot of other illegal nonsense. When the senator got the video I understand he was quite upset."

"Once upon a time the politician would have been forced to leave office."

"Nowadays it does not happen. The lackey gets put to the sword. It is a sacrifice the politician is willing to make."

"Woe is the lackey who gets caught."

"Anyway, Pamela is most unhappy and unemployed. But Vicky is happy."

"The world is right again."

"Right enough."

"She thinks a lot of you."

"I believe she is quite a woman. Question is, what does she think of you?"

"I'm not sure, but we will explore that over another dinner tomorrow night."

"Uh oh, the forces of darkness congeal."

"I'm not sure I like that metaphor. Congeal makes me think of solidified fat on top of cold soup."

"When you put it like that, I agree it is not appealing.

Please change my congeal to converge, with a slight percentage of congeal still active."

"Whatever. I thought it best to go out and see if we hit it off."

"For what it is worth, and you definitely don't need my approval, but I approve."

"Thanks. Whatever happens is your fault anyway, for sending her my direction."

"Obviously I was not thinking clearly. But make sure she gives you your dollar back. You don't want to get into trouble for fraternizing with a client."

"You know that does not matter since I can't take clients. And I already spent the dollar to put air in my tires."

"Is that what they call it nowadays?"

"Remove your smirk and your mind from the gutter."

"Will do. About time she had some good luck. Tell her I said hello."

"I will. You know, thinking about your buddy Ben, it is funny how a crook tries to hide something. Puts it almost in the open, but just beyond what most people would look for."

"Maybe that is the best way to hide something. Or maybe if they are a narcissist, they want people to know, or at least suspect."

"That is why lawyers will always be in business. People just keep being people."

"I guess. When can you get your license back?"

"I can apply in five years. But I won't. Talk to you later."

"Bye."

I turned around and went back to the Cove. I had a hunch about something. I picked Sam up at his house and we went to the barn where the truck was hidden.

"Sam, can we get this truck up on a rack? I'm curious about something."

"Obviously there is not a lift around here. But we can build a temporary one with the timbers and beams in the back of the barn. Why do you want to lift it?"

"Lester was out of money. But he still kept his cars. Even though the tracker you found was old, I bet he still paid for a subscription to keep it active. It is a nice antique, but it isn't that valuable."

"I don't know, but I understand what you are thinking. What are you hoping to find?"

"I have no idea. But I'd like to check."

"I'm interested enough to build a platform."

"I'll help."

It took some effort to build up a platform from the unused beams that would get the truck about three feet up safely. We had enough heavy boards to build a ramp to the platform that the truck could handle. After that it was easy to drive it onto the platform. All we needed were two good flashlights and time. Scrunching down to get under the truck was a little uncomfortable.

"Sam, I think we should have built the platform higher."

"We could have. But the beams that were left were mostly rotten. The truck would have fallen on us."

"I guess that would have been a potential downside."

"Uncomfortable or dead from a crushed head. I'll take uncomfortable."

"Me too. You see anything?" Sam was at the front under the engine, on his knees. I was at the back under the tailgate, sitting on the straw we had put on top of the concrete as padding. My knees were too bad to be on them, but the other part of me was complaining as well.

"Not yet. Other than noticing how simple but well-built these old trucks were. No wonder they lasted so long."

"Funny how technology has made nearly everything so disposable. Make payments on a car for four years, then get a new one before the current one dies."

"Four? Lots of guys are paying on the trucks now for seven years. The contract lasts longer than the truck."

"Sounds crazy, but that is progress."

"Progress for the people selling them or financing them, maybe. You got anything yet?"

"Nothing for sure." We slowly made our way to the middle of the truck.

"James, I didn't see anything obvious. We should take a look at the interior. If nothing is in there, we will have to start taking the truck apart. I'm not sure it is worth it."

"I know what you mean. Come back here and take a look at something I noticed." I slid back toward the gas tank. "You see that metal plate?"

"Yes, looks like the rest of everything under here. Thick metal in good shape with a light rust coating."

"But the bolt heads holding it on are either newer than the metal plate, or they have been taken off more recently. They are shinier than the other bolts and fasteners under here."

"I see it. Let me get a ratchet and we'll take that off."

Five minutes later the plate was off. A thick plastic bag fell out.

"Huh," I said. I tend to be articulate when surprised.

"James, that is a chunk of money lying there."

"It is. Lester had his own bank vault, probably for his illegal money."

"He probably could not trust anyone to keep it for him."

"Sam, how many cars did Lester have?"

"A few. He drove a nice old Cadillac most of the time. This truck sometimes on a Saturday."

"What do you think will happen to his cars?"

"I believe he owes money on them. I doubt he willed them to anybody. Most likely they will end up at a local auction."

"Have you ever wanted an old Cadillac?"

"Until about two minutes ago I would have said no. But the idea is rapidly growing on me."

"Could be a way of recovering some of the money Lester stole from you a long time ago."

"I believe it might."

"I am going to put the plate back on and then we can get the truck down."

"What should we do with this money?"

"I have an idea. Ever heard of 'finders keepers'?"

"I have."

"Let's finish up here and go talk to Irene. Besides, I want to be present when you convince her you need to buy an old Caddy."

"I still don't know what we should do with the truck."

"I have an idea, but will wait until we see Irene."

We were on the back deck watching leaves fall and could now see a few glints of the Flint River off to the side.

"Sam and Irene, are either of you artistic?"

"In what way?" Irene asked.

"Drawing or painting."

"I'm not, but Irene is," Sam said. "Why?"

"I have a project I'd like us to tackle. It would solve a couple of problems at one time."

"What are you thinking?" Irene asked.

Some days later the three of us waited on the road through the Cove. We saw Duffy pushing his empty cart along the road toward us. I was going to ask him someday what he did with the cart.

Duffy wore a confused look as he approached. But he could not take his eyes off the truck. The 1958 Ford pickup, formerly blue, was now painted like a feathered bird. Feathers all over, except the hood, which was painted to look like an arrowhead. Nobody would suspect Lester's truck was under there, somewhere. Well, at least nobody in the Cove was going to say anything.

"Duffy, we decided to find the truck a good home," Irene said. "But it needed something, so we changed the appearance."

"That is one fine-looking truck, Miss Irene."

"The best home we could find for it is right here in the Cove," Sam said. "Duffy, we would like for you to have it."

"Oh yes, yes, please. But I don't have the drink for it."

"Sam and Dunder will put a tank at your place." I said. "They will keep the big tank filled up, and all you have to do is add some to this fine truck."

"I like it, a lot. Thank all of you for this."

"It is our way to thank you, Duffy. Please use it as you need. Would you like to drive it now?"

"Oh yes, yes. But my buggy…"

"Sam and I will put it in the back so you can take it with you," I said.

"That is fine, yes, yes."

Duffy drove off slowly after we had put the grocery cart in the back. We had painted the truck and added some realistic rust spots. Rather, Irene had done the painting, leaving Sam and I to add painted rust. We'd got an antique tag using Lottie's contacts with the county DMV. We were still trying to come up with a way to get Duffy a license. As long as he stayed in the Cove he should not have any trouble, anyway. But we wanted Duffy to be able to go to one of his favorite places. Manchester had an observation platform over the train yard. It was one of his preferred hobbies, watching trains. It was the only thing he didn't have in the Cove. Dunder or another Cover normally drove him over to watch the trains once a week. It would be nice if Duffy could go himself since it was not very far.

CHAPTER TWENTY-FOUR

I went to breakfast at the campus cafeteria. The person I wanted to see was already seated and eating. I grabbed a coffee and sat beside Ison. I slid a file over to him.

"Morning Ison. I bear a gift. Here are the goods on Benjamin. I hope this gets some decisive action taken."

"We can hope, but he still has powerful friends in Atlanta. Can I finish my last bites before taking a look?"

"Of course. No hurry at this point. But I should say that I'm certain his friends will no longer be backing him."

"Oh, that is interesting. Give me a moment while I read this." It actually took him about five minutes as he read, then reread the document.

"I think what this implies is that Benjamin was supplying invoices that appear legitimate against this state account. The funds were then transferred to this procurement account. Seems a bit odd, but could be an out-of-date accounting problem. That account then sent out irregular payments to several external accounts. It appears that the payments roughly match the overall amounts of transfers to the procurement account over a two to three month period. Normal time frame, and those mostly match the invoices. I don't see any smoking gun here."

"It only becomes a problem when you study the invoices and also track down the external accounts. First, look at the top invoice."

"It appears that $24,318 dollars was paid last year for new drapes in the auditorium."

"Ison, I went and checked the auditorium. The curtains don't look new."

"You are right. As far as I know, those have been there for 20 years."

"I also had someone let me into the back storage room behind the stage. No new curtains in storage. Now look at the second one."

"It shows $54,672 for floor repair and refinishing at the gymnasium two years ago. But I know the same floor has been there for at least ten years. The only change was when some pickleball lines were painted last year."

"Yep. And all those invoices show a similar pattern. Things were bought or work was done, but none of those items exist nor was any work done. But the only people that would know that are a few people on campus, none of whom would normally see these accounts."

"That is a big problem. But where did the money go?"

"I had some help with that. That one external account belongs to a shell corporation. But I know who set it up. It belongs to a state senator. The next external account goes to a different shell company. One that is owned by Benjamin Rawley's other shell corporation. Another one is to the currently incarcerated former sheriff, Jefferson Jackson."

"James, I do believe this will end Benjamin's employment. I may need to get a forensic accountant involved to verify the state accounts. But that should not take more than a few days."

"Can that happen without Benjamin's knowledge? I don't want him to find out and hide evidence."

"It can happen without him knowing. I'll get right on this."

"Good, the faster Benjamin is gone the better. His Atlanta protection is already gone."

"I don't know how you got this stuff, but it is good. But was it done illegally?

"Nope. Just had a friend who knows about these financial things run down the accounts and business ownership. The only grey area is how the campus accounts were accessed. But I believe uncovering the excessive fraud outweighs the minor sin of how the data was gathered."

"Great, now I will feel better. But one question. Why was Benjamin paying the former sheriff before he went to jail?"

"I have no idea. But an even better question is why is he still paying him?"

"Oh yes, that is interesting."

I left the cafeteria and rode my bike over to the hospital. I did not know the coroner but did know his apprentice. She might not tell me much but I needed to find out more about the autopsy report. Something I remembered from my visit at the billboard yard had erupted from my brain ooze while I was taking a shower.

"Doc, is Lester's body still in custody?"

I had found Dr. Hoffman in her office. She was taking a few minutes for lunch and did not look happy at my presence.

"James, do you know how rarely I get to eat lunch these days? Now you want to talk about a body."

"Sorry to bother you, but I have this final issue to figure out."

"This better be good."

"I tell you what, if you help me out, I'll bring you lunch the rest of the week."

"That is a deal. OK, Lester's body was released to the funeral home, and they were trying to locate family. Not much if any family was left and nobody wanted the body because they didn't want to pay for a funeral or cremation."

"Can you take another look at it? Maybe today if you have time?"

"I can call and find out."

"Please do, this might be important."

"Give me a moment." She went outside in the hall to make the call. When she came back, I could tell from her face it was bad news.

"He was cremated yesterday."

"Oh. What about blood samples?"

"Probably already gone. The autopsy findings clearly showed heart attack with no evidence of assault or injury, and the toxicology reports were clear. It was classified as a natural death at the time. But those results were not released to the public because of how the body was found and questions around it. But the lab would have gotten the release to dump samples after the natural cause finding."

"Would elevated epinephrine levels have shown up in the blood?"

"Probably. But that would not have been on the standard test panel. Why?"

"Do you have photographs of the body? Or do you remember any places that looked like bug bites or bee stings?"

"I think there was something on his back, but don't recall the details. I have photographs in my training file since the corner gave me copies. I'll get them out of the file cabinet."

A minute later she had the file on her desk. She read a few notes and then selected a photograph showing Lester's upper back.

"There were three bug bites, possibly bee stings, on the left side of the back just under the shoulder blade in the fleshy part of the back. But we checked for anaphylactic shock and there was no evidence. No causation between the bites and the heart attack."

"I don't believe it was only a heart attack."

"But clearly the heart had burst open. What would cause that?"

"What about multiple doses of injected epinephrine?"

"Yes, that would likely result in heart attack at his age."

"Those three spots look like an equilateral triangle."

"Yes."

"Do you have three epinephrine injectors handy?"

"They are in the dispensary. I can go check them out."

"I would appreciate it. I'd like to measure the needle points while they are held together in one hand."

When she got back, she had three injectors and a ruler. We measured the distance between the points when all three were held together. She also measured the three "bites" on the photograph as there was a scale on each picture.

"The pattern matches, as well as the distances between the three needle points. James, this means Lester was murdered."

"Maybe, or maybe not. This is circumstantial evidence. Without a body or samples for further testing it can't be confirmed. So, no weapon. And without a confession or compelling evidence, there is no suspect either."

"Which means no case."

"No, at least not one I can think of. Cause of death is still the heart attack, but there is some question in my mind that it could have been induced."

"Mine too. What are you going to do?"

"Probably nothing. What about you?"

"I will mention it to the coroner. But as you said, without confirmation it is just a possibility."

"Thanks for indulging my curiosity, Doc."

"Thank you for making my life more complicated, James."

"Happy to oblige. I'll see you tomorrow when I drop off lunch."

I had not told Dr. Hoffman the entire truth. I did have a good suspect, even if I could not prove it. Who had a stash if epinephrine injectors besides the hospital and Charles Robinson? I now had enough evidence to convince myself that Charles killed Lester. Now I needed a reason for him to have done it. Or rather, why him and not the other two thousand people that hated Lester.

After leaving the hospital and pedaling to the bookstore,

my phone rang. Riding a bike and talking on the phone was not conducive to my health. I saw lots of riders do it in the Netherlands but they had lived most of their lives on bikes. I had no intention of ending mine by answering the call.

I parked the grey ghost bicycle and checked the phone. It was a call worth returning. She was my first wife's daughter in England, and we kept in touch after my visit there to help find out what happened to her stepfather. After three rings Elizabeth picked up.

"Hi James."

"Hey Elizabeth, how are you?"

"Very good, thank you."

"How is uni?"

"Now that I have caught up, it is great. That is why I called. I got into the internship and work program. This summer I'll be in Amsterdam at the Rijksmuseum as an intern. The following summer I'll return as a temporary employee."

"That's wonderful, Elizabeth."

"I think so too. A lot. Mum and I are going over for a few days at Christmas to look at the museum and the area. We need to find a few areas where I can find a short-term flat."

"I'm sure you will enjoy the museum and the city. Plenty of things to do when you aren't working."

"Mum will come over for two weeks in the summer. But I wanted to invite you over."

"Only if you mom will be there at the same time. Amsterdam is a nice place to go on dates." The phone was silent. "Elizabeth, I'm joking." I finally heard laughter.

"That is a sick sense of humor. I like you both, but I just don't see you ever being together."

"Of course not, and something we realized decades ago. But I'm glad you got what you wanted. The Rijksmuseum will be a fantastic place to learn."

"I am looking forward to it. Do you think you can come over?"

"I will. I don't know exactly when, of course, but I'm due to visit Amsterdam."

"That sounds great."

"How has everything else been going?"

"Mum has been busy. Ian seems happy but has been spending a lot of time at uni. I think he has a girlfriend."

"How are you and Olivia getting along?"

"Things have been good. We have a bit of our own lives to lead now, so when we do see each other we don't fight."

"I'm glad to hear it. Do tell her I said hello."

"I shall. I'll look forward to the summer."

"Me too."

CHAPTER TWENTY-FIVE

"You must be relieved since you no longer have to investigate a murder," Bryan said. He had come over from next door.

"I am. But it has been rewarding. I've learned about the Cove and met some new people." I was going to draw out telling him about the newest findings. Or the late-night phone call I had gotten from Dunder, revealing new details. Plus my trip this morning back to visit the antenna dish.

"Then it has not been a waste of time. Maybe this happened for a reason, and you are now going to write a book on the history of the Cove."

"Not me. That would be a lot of work. I have neglected my typical hours of sitting on the porch. But I did uncover Lester's murderer."

"That would be a neat trick since he died from a heart attack."

"He did have a heart attack. That was the two the murder was committed."

"You may need to explain that further."

"I think it was induced."

"So who did it?"

"The brief summary is that Lester Owens was killed by Charles Robinson. Charles' parents came to Woodbury because his father was hired as a supervisor at the Owen's pimento plant. He found some significant safety issues there and tried to fix them. But the Owens family refused to spend the money and fired him when he persisted. Lester held the Robinson's mortgage loan. He possibly forged it so they had to pay it all at once or lose the house. They left in a lot worse financial shape than they arrived. Something else happened that day, causing Mr. Robinson to physically throw Lester off the porch, according to stories. Charles was a boy in the middle of all that."

"That is a good motive. What was the weapon?"

"There were three bug bites or small stings on Lester's back just below his shoulder blade. The coroner noted it but it was not considered material to the case. Nobody dies from bug bites, nor is there any indication of anaphylactic shock from any stings. Even if they were injection sites, no drugs were found in his body. But if you hold three epinephrine injectors together in your hand, it gives the exact pattern seen on Lester's back."

"Would that have caused Lester's heart attack?"

"Likely. Someone Lester's age could have his heart explode just like the coroner found. Charles has a stash of epinephrine injectors at his office and at the billboard yard. Apparently, it is a workplace hazard, as his employees often encounter wasp and hornet nests."

"But what was the idea behind putting him up on the dish?"

"I think Charles wanted to stage it as an accident. Make it look like Lester climbed up the dish to write something stupid and had his heart attack while up there. Charles put Lester there to humiliate him in death. That way, Charles got his revenge through murder while staging it as an accident. But then publicly showing what a clown Lester was. And it was all done in the Cove. The place where Lester had harmed Charles' family."

"That is a pretty good way of killing someone and making the most of both a show of the body and a coverup of the murder. But what about the missing truck? Hard to explain how Lester got there, throwing doubt on the accident theory. Seems like an unforced error on Charles' part."

"Lester's truck was parked by the road in front of the dish complex that night. It was supposed to be there when the body was found."

"Then it must have been stolen as the sheriff thought. But I still have not seen any report about a stolen vehicle."

"This is where it gets a little tricky for me. A black ladder truck towed the pickup to the dish. It turns out a good Samaritan moved the truck in an effort to give it to someone else. The someone else who received the truck thought they were being framed for Lester's murder and hid the truck. So it nearly threw a wrench in Charles' plan."

"How do you know there was a black ladder truck on site that night?"

"Oh, uh, the person who moved Lester's truck saw the ladder truck there."

"What, you have knowledge there was an eyewitness present that night?"

"Remember me telling you there was a tricky part? There was someone there, but he is not going to be a credible witness."

"I imagine the prosecutor would think otherwise."

"No, probably just the opposite. The witness told me about the black ladder truck by describing it as a big black locomotive with a train track inside it."

"It was a child? What were they doing out there at night?"

"Wasn't a child. It was a full-grown man."

"Really? Oh, I think I know who you are talking about. Yeah, you are right. The prosecutor would not put him on the stand. Did that guy really see everything?"

"No, only part of it. What he did see was a black truck towing Lester's truck, then the ladder going up to the dish. He saw someone carrying something up the ladder, along with a bucket. Once they came down, they drove off. After that he came down off the other dish and decided to take Lester's truck and leave it with someone that had been nice to him."

"Are you going to tell me about those third parties?"

"I'm not sure. In fact, I'm not sure to whom in law enforcement I should tell this story. John Dixon, I guess, since it is his jurisdiction. It all fits together, but it is all circumstantial. Might as well make the interim sheriff's life more difficult. What do you think so far?"

"The missing truck is important as a piece to finish the

story. But it is not relevant to the actual murder or the coverup as I see it."

"That is what I thought."

"You do have a suspect, a motive, and a weapon. Enough to consider opening an investigation of Charles, I believe."

"Just consider? Are you saying that if it is not strong enough, the sheriff might not even take it to the next level?"

"Exactly. Prosecutors want the easiest case possible to give them a sure win and make them look good. A weak case against someone held in regard in the community might not get prosecuted, depending on the circumstances of the case and the victim. Lester was not exactly loved in the community."

"I understand. I did all I could to put the case together, but I certainly don't have a confession from Charles Robinson."

"Plus, you might have to identify who moved the truck and who hid it. They will definitely be pulled in as witnesses and potentially prosecuted for tampering with evidence."

"I know. You are not helping convince me to go forward."

"You could tell John what you told me. If the missing truck comes up, feign ignorance. Meanwhile, somebody has to come up with a reasonable explanation of where the truck is and how it got there, or it should disappear forever."

"True. But what about the ladder truck? I bet Lester's DNA would be on it. Charles has only two ladder trucks, a silver and a black. The black one was the one that put him on the dish. I know the truck put Lester there, because I went back out and found two rub marks on the edge of the dish. The measured distance between the marks matches the truck ladder."

"First of all, even if Lester's DNA was on the truck, I would bet not only Charles' but also his entire crew's DNA would also be present. Second, that does not prove anything regarding murder, just the misdemeanor charge of desecrating remains. Someone might even claim Lester, while alive, paid to have the truck there to get him up on the dish, then he had the heart attack. You know John is already considering that the corpse was moved, but it was not murder."

"I'll have to think about everything and then decide what to do. Thanks for listening and the analysis. Now, a change of topic. I have a reliable source that thinks the other person in Doyle's truck the night of Mike's murder was Deputy Deacon."

"Now that is interesting. An eyewitness?"

"Unfortunately, no. A very educated guess."

"I can guess who made that guess. But it might be something to use against Deacon to get him to rat out the sheriff. But since they are both in jail for some years, he still might not flip on former Sheriff Jackson."

"But maybe worth a try. I'd feel better if the sheriff stayed locked up during my lifetime."

"I know the feeling. But I'm sure he will be properly rehabilitated once he gets out."

"More like he will have constructed a better system to move his drugs."

"I assume you are concerned that he will miss his buried rewards."

"I wish the other septic tanks full of cash would show up. No reason to give him any help once he gets out."

"Give that puzzle to Millard's gang. The ones you call the Octoposse."

"Not a bad idea. Considering the potential financial reward, I think they will jump at the chance to find them."

"See, your day is already brighter. You are going to have to forget about Charles and Lester."

"Lester will be easy to forget. Charles, however, will not."

"You have a devious mind. I'm sure you can come up with something."

"I just might, Bryan, I just might."

After Bryan left, I walked the campus loop to see Millard. He was on his porch as usual, soaking up the late afternoon sun.

"Hey Millard, I know who killed Lester Owens."

"I do too. It was the Grim Reaper."

"I hope you had a bet on him."

"Nope, he doesn't count. He technically gets credit for everybody."

"Anyway, it was not him. Plain old murder."

"Really? Has anyone been arrested?"

"I don't know what is happening with any arrests or prosecutions. Not my concern, but I am confident I know the murderer."

"So tell me who it was."

"Charles Robinson. Was he in your suspect pool or betting matrix? "

"The name does sound familiar. Let me take a look at the spreadsheet. Yep, he is on it. A real long shot. Oh, Lottie put in a late bet on Charles not long ago. She is going to win quite a pot if you are right."

I laughed to myself. I was sure she had placed that bet

right after I had asked her to look into Charles Robinson. A little insider trading.

"She's a lucky woman, Millard."

"She certainly is."

I doubted we were referring to the same thing.

"Tell me what you know about Lester's murder," Millard said.

I went through a similar version that I had told Bryan earlier. "What do you think, Millard?"

"That is quite a tale. And no, it would probably not be brought to court. Again, it only points to corpse desecration, not murder. But you've already gone through all this yourself, haven't you?"

"I have, but I wanted you to hear it and work through the possibilities. Maybe see something I have not."

"Wait a minute, what about the blood? Was it not from Lester?"

"It was deer blood."

"Easy enough to get around here this time of year."

"It is. I know one processor that has deer's blood in a drum behind his operation. It gets picked up once a week along with all the other yucky stuff. There is no security on it since nobody wants to steal blood. I suppose Charles used deer's blood since it would not be traceable. He did not want to use paint that could be traced to him. He knows about that from his business."

"Overall, the story is compelling, but I doubt there is enough to convict. More importantly, the jury will come from Hamilton County. Any of them who knew Lester probably hated him and would thank his murderer. Even displaying the corpse would just get a laugh, not a conviction. The prosecutor will know that too."

"So Charles gets away with murder."

"Very likely. Short of a confession or concrete evidence you have not found, I don't think there is any chance of a conviction."

"A confession won't happen, and I've nothing left to investigate."

"Not every criminal gets prosecuted."

"And sometimes an innocent person does. The old adage that life is not fair."

"True, unfortunately. Speaking of criminals, I saw you the other day at the golf course garden. Seemed to be looking for something with the fancy equipment."

"Yes, some archaeology graduate students brought their equipment. I thought it would help narrow down where I needed to dig."

"Did it help?"

"Quite a bit. I recovered a few teeth, a piece if skull, and what might be a pocket watch."

"Then your letter was accurate. Now you have an ancient, and possibly unsolvable murder mystery to unravel."

"I suppose so. But this one has been dormant for 80 years, so there's no rush to solve it."

"Take your time. But remember, us elderly folks would like to know before our demise."

"I'll keep that in mind."

CHAPTER TWENTY-SIX

"There is nobody listening," I said. "I'm not wearing a recording device and there is no one in the bushes with one of those recording cones. Just you and me having a conversation. If you don't believe me we can walk around somewhere else and you can search me."

I was sitting with Charles Robinson on a bench on the grounds of the Little White House. Well away from the buildings and the few tourists walking around on a beautiful fall day. I had coerced him to meet me.

"I don't think I need to do that," he said. "What do you want to talk about?"

"I know what you did and how you did it. No reason to go back over any of that."

"I don't know what you mean."

"Yeah, you do. What I want to know is the why. I have a

pretty good idea of the general facts. But the details make all the difference."

"Maybe they do. But I won't tell you."

"Why don't you start out by giving me some hypothetical scenarios? Tell me what could have happened, like we were trying to come up with a book plot."

"If you are not recording us, why do you want to know?"

"Professional curiosity. Most of the time I never get the complete story. Also, other people are involved in other aspects of the incident and I need to protect them."

"I'll tell you what really happened in the Cove many years ago. Then maybe I'll talk about more recent hypothetical happenings."

"Fair enough."

"I'm sure you know my family came here because my father was going to supervise the Owen's pimento canning plant. He was good at what he did and made the place more profitable over the first three or four years. But he was also a stickler for safety. He worried about the equipment wearing out and company policies to not replace anything, and began advocating for safety practices. Previously he had been at another plant when a canner blew up. The nearby workers that survived the initial blast got hit with steam. Their skin sloughed right off, and they died agonizing deaths after a few days. So he wanted things done right. The Owen's family did not want the loss of profit from shutting any canners down for maintenance or replace them.

"After a lot of turmoil they fired him. Guards pushed him out the door. I was at home when he arrived from work that day and he and mom started talking. But that wasn't the worst of it. They had bought the house we lived in from

Lester. But he put a clause in the contract that it was a rent-to-own property the first ten years, and he could force them out at any time unless they paid it off. Dinner time came and Lester drove up. Told my folks they had to leave. They did not believe him but he had the contract. Whether it was a clause in the original contract or he later forged it, I don't know. But my folks knew the Owen's family ran Woodbury, and the law was on their side.

"Then Lester said something I didn't understand until I was older. It made my dad so mad he threw Lester off the porch. The next morning my father got a truck, and we started packing up the house. We left that night and stayed in Macon. The next day we were in Savannah at my grandparent's house. Dad got a job at a seafood plant and we eventually got another house.

"I measure my early life by the time we lived in the Cove and the time after the Cove. Before that, we were all happy. My parents did not fight or brood. But after that they fought and eventually stopped talking to each other. The summer I finished high school they divorced, and it was not amicable."

"What did Lester say to make your dad throw him out?"

"He said we could stay if he could have my mom."

"Wow, that was horrible thing to say."

"Now you know why my father did what he did."

"What about more recent events?"

"I moved back here and opened my business. It has been good. I saw Lester a few times around but he did not know who I was."

"That must have changed."

"Hypothetically, there might have been plans to do something about him. But he was old and everybody hated him.

They didn't want to be around him. Funny how that happened after he ran out of money. It seemed an appropriate punishment. But one day, hypothetically, a decision was made to confront him about the past. Took him a while to understand and remember those events. Instead of denying his actions or feeling remorse, he said some more terrible things. Hypothetically, even though it was not planned, his mouth caused a reflex action. Another party's hand just kind of reacted on its own and you probably know what was in the hand."

"You just happened to have three in your hand at the time?"

"There actually were six as I was stocking a truck. I was mad enough that I hit my truck first, and that knocked off three caps. I don't think I'll say anymore."

"For what it is worth, I believe you."

"What happens now? You take the case to the sheriff?"

"I can't, or rather I won't. The way this all came about, other people are involved you know nothing about. Some of it goes back to before your time in the Cove. If this comes out, they get hurt. Lester was such a negative influence around here for so long that his sins still cause problems. They don't need to get hurt again."

"I understand. Thanks for not turning me in. Can I ask you a question?"

"Sure."

"What happened to the truck?"

"Let's just say it was re-gifted."

"Oh."

"Can I ask you a question? Do you feel guilty?"

"It has been very strange. Sometimes the guilt eats at me.

Yet I don't regret what happened to Lester. But the guilt comes because I did it. Even though I won't pay for what I did, I still have to live with it."

"Oh, I never said you were getting away free and clear. Just that I would not turn you in."

"Of course. Now you are going to blackmail me. What do you want?"

"This is what I want you to do. First of all, I am going to give you a bag of cash..."

Things were not right, nor just. Lester had reigned over Woodbury for too long, bringing misery to too many. Things would never be as right as they should be, but I thought they were better. And I had the rest of my life to ponder whether justice could be done without the law's involvement. I hoped so because I knew the law sometimes was enacted on people without justice. Maybe the whole Lester saga ended with its own version of justice. As for me, right or wrong, I had made decisions I would have to live with. Charles wasn't going to jail, but he had penance to do. But didn't we all?

Lester got what he probably deserved. I had never met him but all the stories pointed to a person that was better out of the community. Charles had his conscience to deal with, plus the new deeds I required of him. Sam and Irene were the proud owners of an old Cadillac and had recovered some of the money Lester had stolen from them. Dunder had bought Lester's other old car and recovered some of his money. I had called Atlanta, and they had called off my watcher. They had also granted another request. I now owed them a favor.

As for me, a few weeks later, I was finally free from investigating and could resume my fall hikes up Pine Mountain.

Today as I began my walk, the silvery light from the sunlit fog perfused the campus. I didn't know if there was a word for a silver version of sepia, but that is what this was. It did not happen very often but when it did, the light was magical. In the woods the light changed. It did not glow as much since the fog was dispersed in the trees. But the silver shine from the wet leaves made up for it. I walked up for an hour and then down. It was an auspicious start for the fall hiking season.

To finish, I hiked the level outer loop on campus. Millard was out in the yard checking in the slow-growing magnolias I had transplanted for him. He waved me up.

"Did you hear about Charles Robinson?" he asked. "He set up a trust to fund the disadvantaged in the Cove. Even covers a college scholarship in Lagrange. Looks like people there will get the help they need. I wonder what possessed him to do that?"

"Who knows? He must be a good guy."

"Uh huh. Did you hear who was on the new Cove board? Your friends Sam and Irene, plus Dunder and Charles. Interesting how they got together."

"It is for the good of the Cove. I'm glad it is happening."

"Me too. Do you have anything else to add?"

"Nope."

"You really are a sneaky sort."

"I learned from my elders. You and Lottie, especially."

"I'll take that as a compliment. How did you manage it?"

"The best form of blackmail is getting someone to do what they are already inclined to do."

"Yep, just as I thought. Sneaky."

When I neared home, I saw a familiar black-clad figure waiting for me at my house. I had been expecting her.

"James, what is this?" Sabrina asked. "What have you done?"

"I don't know Sabrina. What are we talking about?"

"This right here." She took an envelope from her pocket and handed it to me.

"What do you want me to do with this?"

"Read it and tell me if this was you."

"Why don't you just tell me what it says?"

"It is a scholarship offer from Lagrange College. Something about the Robinson fund."

"I have to say that is convenient. If someone were inclined to go to college, that is."

"It was you, wasn't it?"

"I believe you said it was Robinson somebody. Maybe you should talk to him."

"I know who he is. The one you tracked down for the murder on the dish."

"I believe that is true."

"Why are you interfering in my life?"

"Sabrina, this is merely an option. You have to decide whether to take it or not. Only you can make that decision. If you don't want it, don't go. If you do want it, the Atlanta family has already given permission. Your choice."

She hugged me quickly and left without saying anything else. I imagine she was surprised and confused. I really could not tell what she was going to do. But it was now her choice, and she had an option to change her life. Even then, she could go to school and return to her old life. I knew that if she went to school, though, she'd not return to the family. I suspected she knew it as well.

There was nothing more I could do, nor anything I should do to try to sway her. I would keep in touch as best I could as I wanted to know her decision.

I had a call to make to continue the old letter investigation. Perhaps now was a good time to find out all I could on the principals involved. Now I had the letter along with a small batch of human remains that seemed to confine the events.

Donna picked up the call after the first ring. "Hi James. I enjoyed lunch last week."

"Me too."

"Have all the rest of your plans worked out yet?"

"Mostly. Some things are possibly more rightish than before."

"That is all you can do. Are you going to tell me all about it?"

"I will. I think our car ride to Atlanta and a followup trip to New York should give me plenty of time to tell you everything."

"That is presumptuous of you. Or have you found out more about the events from your old letter?"

"I have found out more. I even have a bag of teeth to prove it."

"Well, it is nearly Halloween. When do we leave?"

"A few things to do first. But if you are game, maybe in November. Before I fly out to northern California to see my son."

"I should be able to make that work."

"Lottie and Millard, I have to say this is a surprise," I said.

"But do you like it?" Lottie asked.

"Well, I think so. It is just not what I imagined. Not at all. How did you come up with it?"

"It went to the committee. The one you call the Octoposse. A few dozen rounds of discussion and voting, and this was what came out."

"Interesting."

"But do you like it?"

"I think so. No, I know I do. I really appreciate the time and effort you both put into choosing it." I looked up at the new sign again.

Wilder Things Bookstore. I guess it was appropriate, all things considered. A play on my name, plus close to one of the most famous children's books of all time. And if Millard kept sneaking his poker games into the back room, it would be wild. I had already heard the Octoposse meetings got rowdy when someone won a big betting pool.

"We are having a grand re-opening next weekend," Lottie said. "Food, drink, live music, the newspaper reporter, everything. Are you up for it?"

"Yes, I am. You know, maybe we should have an author or two here as well. We need to support the local folks."

"Already booked."

"Who did you get?"

"Who do you think? You are being dense again. She was the first author at the old store. Makes sense she is the first for the grand opening of the new store."

"Donna is going to do it?"

"Of course. Said she was honored and would not miss it."

"Huh."

"So what do you think about her being here?"

"I think she is a good choice."

"Just you remember that, James."

"I will. We still on for pickleball tonight?"

"Would not miss it."

* * *

The End
of
Body in the Cove
but not the Warm Springs Mystery series

AUTHOR'S NOTES

The Roosevelt Warm Springs, or RWS campus exists mostly as described. A few liberties were taken with details. For example, there is an abandoned camp on site by the lake, but it was not a Boy Scout retreat.

Similarly, the town of Warm Springs is mostly as described. Unfortunately, Mable's Diner does not exist and to my knowledge never has. Other restaurants and stores are there, however.

A significant change I made was to create the fictitious Hamilton County. It was carved from the actual counties of Meriwether, Harris, Troup and Talbot. The new county includes the towns of Warm Springs, Manchester, Pine Mountain, Shiloh, Woodland, and Hamilton, plus most of the ridge of Pine Mountain, and all of Roosevelt State Park. It was done to simplify jurisdictions of the towns, state park and RWS campus. I made the county seat the town of Hamilton. It is a real county seat, but for Harris County.

The Cove is a real place. Its description as a crater is appropriate. The large dish antennae included in the book are there as described. Stories about the Cove can be heard across the region, but little written history is available. It is worth a drive down the one road across it.

The Roosevelt Warm Springs campus and the town of Warm Springs are worth a visit, as well as the Little White House. All were amazing places in the time of Franklin D. Roosevelt, and hopefully the RWS campus will be again.

Kat does exist and will welcome visitors. Kat is not her real name—I've used a pen name for her to protect her true identity. But if you see a fluffy tabico miniature Maine Coon cat eyeing chipmunks in front of the house, you'll know it's her.

ABOUT THE AUTHOR

I'm D. Smith, a native Georgian that can't seem to stay in the state for long. Tried a number of states and Europe so far, and lately have settled in Asheville, North Carolina. But I do now have a house on the Roosevelt Warm Springs campus, so soon that will be home.

I've been a lot of things over my work career, but I've put that nonsense behind me. The travel in America, Europe, and Asia was useful as an author. And finally the Ph.D. came in useful—for writing about food.

I now write books and pet cats for fun, since neither pays very well. I'm weaning myself away from social media, but the links below give a little more background and perhaps foreground on the author known as D. Smith.

RECIPE

SIMPLE PASTA

Ever had an old, worn dish of bland food? Then tried a simpler version, with fresh ingredients, that is simply incredible? This is the recipe to turn boring pasta into vibrant bites everyone at dinner will remember. The origin of this recipe came from a small restaurant in Verona, Italy. Most every serving of food there was simple, fresh, and fantastic. And yet so easy to prepare at home. Try it once and wow yourself. The next time, serve to guests with a nice wine, or iced tea. As shown below, it can be made with as few as four ingredients, plus salt.

The Ingredients
    Pasta, 16 oz box of linguine
    Pine nuts, a handful
    Sun-dried tomatoes, 8 oz jar in olive oil
    Olive oil
    Flaked Parmesan or Manchego cheese (optional)
    Balsamic vinegar (optional)

The Process

Pasta:

Add just enough water to cover the pasta noodles in the pot. Begin to boil, and add salt to taste. After a few minutes reduce heat and keep stirring to allow all the water to evaporate, but keep the noodles from sticking to the bottom of the pan. Once the noodles are almost tender according to your preference, add 1/4 cup of half and half or similar product. Reduce heat and keep stirring another one to two minutes to allow the dairy to absorb. Check salt level again as more might be needed.

Topping:

Use a larger pan because the pasta will go into it at the end. Sauté the pine nuts in olive oil (enough to cover the bottom of the pan) on medium heat. The pine nuts need to fry just enough to get a little color. Add the tomatoes. Continue stirring and add a couple of tablespoons of balsamic vinegar if the tomatoes are bland. Don't overcook and fragment the tomatoes.

Add pasta to the sauté pan and keep on heat another two minutes while stirring. The flavored oil needs to thoroughly coat the pasta. Add salt to taste. Add cheese if preferred.

Toss on a plate and commence to eating.

Finishing Notes

Pasta will absorb about anything. If half and half is not available, try milk, cream, or broth. Or nothing at all.

Sprinkle with a good cheese if desired, but be aware it can detract from the other flavors. To add something different, drop fresh spinach or parsley leaves into the sauté pan for the last minute or so before adding the pasta.

The secret to simple dishes is fresh, high-quality ingredients. If the pine nuts smell musty or taste tangy, or if a few drops of the olive oil taste off, don't use them. They won't improve with cooking.

Note: Most of my recipes are very loose, as I frequently experiment and encourage others to do so. Failures are frequent but can be fun. Keep a fire extinguisher handy.

* 9 7 8 1 9 6 4 3 4 4 0 6 5 *